Previous books by the same author
Melody Beaucello (speculative fiction–Zeus Publications)
Australian Historical Fiction Trilogy–*Pursuit of Happiness,*
Out of the Shadow, Dappled Sunshine–Balboa Press

First Published in 2022 by Echo Books

Echo Books is an imprint of Superscript Publishing Pty Ltd, ABN 76 644 812 395

Registered Office: PO Box 997, Woodend, Victoria, 3442.

www.echobooks.com.au

National Library of Australia Cataloguing-in-Publication entry.

Creator: Florence, Neill, author.

Title: Serendipity Murder: Neill Florence

ISBN: 978-1-922603-81-4 (paperback)

A catalogue record for this book is available from the National Library of Australia

Book and cover design by Peter Gamble, Canberra.
Set in Garamond Premier Pro Light Display, 12/17 and Americanus Regular.

www.echobooks.com.au

Cover image, Shutterstock.

SERENDIPITY MURDER

a novel by
Neill Florence

echo)))
BOOKS

Chapter 1

Serendipity Gardens Retirement Village started life on the edge of Brisbane about 30 years ago, but now in 1995 it shares its suburb with a shopping strip and a super market, an industrial estate and a caravan park, several churches and petrol stations, and street after street of assorted dwellings that classify their owners somewhere on the social continuum between the mega rich and the abjectly poor.

Behind the high walls of Serendipity, however, the classification of people while it is a matter of interest for some of the residents it is not an exercise that can rely for its judgements on the design and upkeep of houses. All the Serendipity cottages are look-alikes and all enjoy a high standard of upkeep that is seen to by the village management. There is no opportunity in the village for one-upmanship through choosing to live in the biggest house although a reference is sometimes made to the number of bedrooms a house has.

None of the residents are overly rich. If they were, they wouldn't have chosen Serendipity Gardens as a venue for their twilight years, but those that did choose Serendipity are by no means impoverished. The poor couldn't afford to live here. You need to be a self-funded retiree or a pensioner with a supportive investment portfolio to back the cost of living the comfortable life on offer here. Any classifying of people that might be done within the Village by people in the Village sorts them out not according to wealth but according to the trades or professions followed before retirement. It's not surprising that retired nurses and teachers, bank managers and accountants, public servants and shop keepers, and successful plumbers and electricians are in good supply in the village.

A few of the residents, however, won't accept that they belong to any sort of middle class, even a prosperous one. They either belong to no class at all or, according to them, they represent the new 20th century aristocracy that is set apart not through hereditary, or new wealth, but through education.

I was talking to one such self-styled aristocrat at a Friday Happy Hour in the Village soon after I arrived here and he spoke to me at great length about the new order in society. I couldn't help smiling at such empty elitism that attempted to confer status on a person just because he or she managed to acquire a university degree, but my smile faded to blank incredulity when he claimed that education at certain grand private schools was equivalent to education at a university as far as status is concerned.

He even talked about the school tie and the school motto as though they were hallowed armorial bearings on their escutcheons. I was no candidate for inclusion in such a snobbish group of lame duck sophisticates so I made my response to his insanity by just staring at him so blankly that I probably gave him the impression that I was the one who was insane. I would give no one the opportunity to classify me as anything but one of the two million human beings currently living in Brisbane.

I had come to Serendipity Gardens determined to reveal nothing of my former life and I don't intend to reveal anything of the ethical or professional reasons for such a decision. I just hope that no one here at Serendipity will ever find out that I was the police inspector who for twenty years managed to hunt down murderers and other criminals operating in Central Queensland and deliver them to their destiny in the Rockhampton Court House. I can't be a complete nonentity here at Serendipity though. If nothing at all is known about me, I will stand out as a man of mystery rather than fade into the background as a man of no particular interest. I have let drop therefore that I was a public servant before I retired and spent my days chatting at the water cooler and filing correspondence that had been dealt with by others, and checking the mountains of forms that piled up in my in-tray before consigning them also to the oblivion of the filing system.

I am quite happy with what I've achieved in life and I have no real need to attract the notice of others, or at least that's what I tell myself knowing full well that it could be disastrous for me to attract attention. Anyway, am I really happy with anonymity when one of my plans for retirement is to produce a book of detective stories based on my Central Queensland cases? Hardly, I suppose, when I'm entertaining the idea that my book will be called *Inspector Coleman's Cadavers*. I have to accept the axiom that the urge to write has the desire to be read as a corollary, but I'm confident that the use of a pseudonym will protect my essential privacy. Frank Coleman will not appear as the author of my book and no one at Serendipity will associate the colourless and retiring Frank Coleman with the protagonist, the high-profile Inspector Coleman, should they stumble on my book if it gets published.

Most importantly one of my earlier cases will not be included in the book. It will stay in the past hiding from cold case scrutiny, and my justification of what I did will stand without any contribution from a judge and jury, or social media scuttlebutt.

Chapter 2

It's Friday morning and I'm sitting on the little back patio of my Serendipity cottage enjoying the warm spring sunshine that has transformed my brave patch of garden into a dazzle of colour. It's one of those years when nature is excelling itself. The petunias alone would have provided a striking enough floral response. Every colour in the petunia palette's getting a splash in the petunia bed, and behind them the purple daises and the white daises are massing together in their clans and they're reaching up on long stems to meet the sunshine. The azalea bushes take the prize though. Since I arrived, they've been sheltering me from my ubiquitous neighbours in staid dark green, but now they've all abandoned decorum and donned bright red gowns.

I'd started to doze, lulled by a surfeit of visual stimulation when my drift to slumber was suddenly confronted by the harsh imposition of disputing voices. My neighbours behind the azaleas were at it again baring their political differences in public. It's been many months since the election and I thought they'd settled down after the long haul of their strident electioneering, but I soon realized that it was Pauline Hanson's maiden speech that had got them going again.

'Hey, Janine, Howard is exposed for the devil he is,' Millie Mockridge shouted to her neighbour, Janine Rumble

'Your rubbish should go to the tip! You're not supposed to keep recycling it,' Janine hit back

'I'm not recycling rubbish. It's in the paper, Pauline Hanson's speech. She wants to kick out the Asians, cut off help for the aboriginals and put-up tariffs to stop us trading with our neighbours!'

'That's got nothing to do with John Howard, you daft Trotskyite. The Liberals expelled her from the party.'

'Howard didn't expel her. He adopted her policies. He's a sodding right-wing conservative. He's never a liberal.

'Rubbish! He's in there for the Aussie battler and his policy is to save the country from the financial mess left by Keating.'

'You're blind as a bat, Janine. You didn't notice that Keating saved the country from becoming a Banana Republic. That took guts.'

'Guts! It took guts to call Australia names and ditch the tariffs that protected our workers? More like graft. He was probably paid by a consortium of overseas factory owners.'

'You liberal camp followers have got your heads stuck deep in the mud. Your party bosses knew that Australia had to become free trade to survive, but they were too chicken to manage the recession the country would have to go through to open it up to the world. Coward Howard will come in now and take all the credit for our prosperity.

'Australia has never prospered under Labour. Of course the Liberals will take the credit when they've cleaned up the mess and returned Australia to the sort of country we had under Menzies.'

I'd had enough. They would carry on mouthing a lot of old clichés that tried to accentuate the differences between two parties whose policies were puffing away along parallel tracks. As I was retreating into my unit, I turned and noticed Jean Reid through the trees. She was standing in her back garden gazing up towards her vigorously argumentative neighbours.

Jean had only moved in last week and I hadn't met her yet. I'd give her time to unpack all her boxes and organize her own comfort before I strolled up and introduced myself. I hoped that the performance she was witnessing wouldn't be giving her any second thoughts about staying. From what I could see of her from my perspective at the other end of our enclosed garden, she seemed like an ideal neighbour. I couldn't even guess at her age, but she carried herself well and she looked intelligent and she was well groomed and attractively dressed. Not that I would fall into the trap of judging a book by its cover, but a book with a strikingly presented cover does stand out from the rest.

Chapter 3

The following Tuesday I was walking back from Ukulele practice in the community room humming some of the old tunes we intended performing in a village concert at the end of the year, songs like *Down by the River Side, The Banks of the Ohio, Botany Bay,* and *Fly Away* (Blue grass style, whatever that is.) They are not tunes I'd normally hum since my disc collection is devoted almost exclusively to Baroque Chamber music. I'd never learnt to play an instrument, but over the years I'd become addicted to the delicious harmonies and perpetual rhythms produced by the string instruments and I'd found that the 17th century composers with their changing moods and contemplative suggestions were the ideal companions to help me draw the curtain on my working day.

The advertisement in the village gossip sheet promised complete satisfaction with the Ukulele for anyone who could hum a tune or tap a foot to a rhythm and I found the promise to be genuine. I could now strum with confidence eight of the 120 odd chords they had on their chart and I knew words to pop songs that I'd ignored when they were topping the charts years ago. Songs like *I'll Walk the Line, and Leaving on a Jet Plane* don't have the rich appeal of Baroque Chamber music, but something happens when you produce all the music yourself. It's like singing in the shower. Every man becomes a Pavarotti when he sings in the shower.

By the time I was entering the shared garden that separated our group of back-to-back cottages, I was actually singing, 'Some bright morning when this life is over, I'll fly away...' I was happy that I'd finally got the tune of the old gospel song and I'd started to sing giving no thought to my surroundings. Jean Reid must have seen me through her security screen because she opened the door and came out onto her patio. She took in the ukulele slung over my shoulder and the song that ceased abruptly as soon as I noticed her, and she came up with her version of what she saw.

'Great, they provide a wandering minstrel at this village to brighten our day with snatches of lilting lullabies.'

I was embarrassed of course, but I tailored a reply to deal with her irony.

'Don't get your hopes up. If I'd fronted up as a minstrel I'd have been sacked after half a dozen chords. I'm learning to be a minstrel, though, thanks to the Ukulele Club. Anyone can learn the Ukulele.'

'No, they can't,' she responded. 'I've got arthritic fingers and I'm tonally challenged.'

'I'm sorry to hear that,' I said.

'There's no need to be sorry for me. I enjoy listening to music, but I'm hopeless at making it myself.'

'Anyway, there are plenty of other things to do here and it's almost obligatory for the residents to join at least one activity to get them mixing even if it's just turning up at a Happy Hour.'

'That's good to know,' she said, 'I find that I've fulfilled my obligation to mix by turning up at last Friday's Happy hour.'

There was a touch of sarcasm in her response and I concluded that the Happy Hour wasn't a happy hour for her.

'You didn't enjoy it,' I said.

'Not really,' she replied. 'I spent the whole hour being asked where I came from and why I'd come. I suppose it was their way of getting to know me.'

I realized that I hadn't introduced myself yet so I went ahead and did it assuring her that my happiness at having her as a neighbour didn't depend on knowing anything about her life before she came to Serendipity. When she started to introduce herself, I said that I already knew who she was because the word about new arrivals gets around a village like this particularly if they've been to a Happy Hour.

'You mightn't really know who I am though,' she said. 'I wouldn't put it past some of them to get even the basic facts wrong.'

'I know that you are Jean Reid and that you come from Queenscliff, but I can easily forget the Queenscliff bit if you want me to.

'No, no. I've no need to erase Queenscliff from my background, but tell me do you know where Queenscliff is?'

'Of course, I'm well-travelled. Queenscliff is a delightful little town at the mouth of Port Phillip Bay full of history and old buildings.'

'Yes, that's Queenscliff. It's starting to change now though. It's been discovered by tourists.'

'A pity, I hope those fishermen's cottages haven't been demolished, and there was a hotel there with the strangest façade.'

'Heritage listing has saved some of the old town,' she said and abruptly dropped the topic.

'Look,' she said, 'would you like a cup of tea?'

I thought she may have wanted to prolong the conversation and I was enjoying talking to her.

'I'd love one,' I said.

Her jiffy jug did its job and she was soon pouring tea at the little table on her back patio and offering me a slice of her generously iced Madeira cake.

'I don't really want to talk about what's going on in Queenscliff,' she said as I stirred the sugar into my tea. 'I want to tell you why I asked you if you knew where Queenscliff is.'

I immediately thought of Roger Masters who held the floor at our last village Philosophy Club meeting. There are only six of us but that doesn't stop us tackling the big questions. Roger claimed that it was the need to know that motivated human beings not the expectation of an afterlife, or the pursuit of happiness, or the desire for moral or ethical outcomes. Did I need to know why Jean Reid asked a simple question?

'Go ahead,' I said. 'I've always had an interest in why people say the things they say.'

She looked at me quickly, I suppose to gauge whether I was being serious or sarcastic elevating her simple statement to an issue for study. She laughed and said,

'Whether you are interested or not, I'm going to tell you why I asked that question. A woman at last Friday's Happy Hour, whose name I didn't catch, asked me the same questions that everybody else did, but it was her reaction to one of my answers that set her apart. If we'd been men, punches would have been thrown.'

'You revealed your allegiance to the wrong political party. Politics and Happy Hours don't mix.'

'No, I'm not a member of any political party. I simply answered her question and said I came from Queenscliff.'

'Ah, Queenscliff is anathema to her and she doesn't trust any of the natives.'

'On the contrary she liked Queenscliff and claimed to have been there, but she started talking about a town that had little resemblance to Queenscliff. When she asserted that my proximity to Queenscliff would make it easy for any family, I still had there to visit me here, I had to point out the misapprehension she seemed to have. I told her that she could hardly say that Queenscliff was just a short journey from Brisbane.'

'Rubbish she replied. 'Just because it's over the border it doesn't mean that it's distant. It's not much further on from the Gold Coast.'

'Queenscliff isn't in New South Wales, it's right down at the bottom of Victoria' I said.

'You are mixed up,' she said. 'How could you live in a town and not even know what state it belongs to?'

'That's not the issue here,' I replied. 'It's your assertion that I don't know where I came from that's strange.

Calling her strange turned her nasty and she shouted at me.

'Strange! What colossal hide! You turn up here and tell the locals that they're strange and argue with them about their local Geography. You are suffering delusions. Serendipity Village is set up for independent living so you'd better move on to a Nursing Home if you are losing your grip on reality.'

With that barb delivered, she turned and marched off leaving me fuming. I left the unhappy Happy Hour and retreated to my unit. When I'd calmed down, I applied some logic to the episode and concluded that there must be two towns in Australia called Queenscliff. I checked my atlas, but only one was listed in the index and that was my Queenscliff at the mouth of Port Phillip Bay.'

There were about 150 people living in our village, but there was only one person that I knew who could have been so dictatorial towards a stranger. I needed to let Jean know that her encounter could be ignored.

'This woman whose name you didn't catch,' I said to her, 'she was shortish and slim with a head of hair that's been organized into the tightest of tight curls by some hairdresser who should have known better because they give way to a face that's angular and severe and carries a default expression that suggests that the milk in the milk bottle she's just sniffed has turned sour.'

'That is an accurate description,' she replied. 'You almost make me feel sorry for her.'

'There's no need to feel sorry for her. She's determined to live up to her name and she ignores any hurt she causes.'

'Live up to her name? What's her name?'

'Martha Setright.'

'You're joking.'

'No, I'm not. She has no idea what is right, but that's her name, and she's attempted to put nearly everyone in the village, including me, in their proper places.

'My proper place is in a Nursing Home apparently. What advice did she have for you?'

'Soon after I arrived, she dressed me down for queue jumping. I went into the auditorium to buy a ticket in a Melbourne Cup sweep that the social committee was organizing. There were two tables, one selling $1 tickets and the other $5 ones. There was a long queue in front of the $1 table and nobody at the other so I decided to buy a $5 ticket and I went straight to that table. Now Martha Setright was on the social committee, which in itself is an oxymoron, and she descended on me and accused me of queue jumping. I protested that there was no queue to jump in front of the $5 table.

She spat back that there was a queue. It went past the $1 table and on to the $5 table because people wanted to buy from both. I told her that I only wanted to buy a $5 ticket and there was no need for me to go past the $1 table first. That really upset her and she shouted at me that I might have got away with organizing things to suit myself in the public service, but I was in the real world now and I was required to consider other people. Her GET BACK INTO THE QUEUE order was so embarrassing that I felt like a dog being called to heel and like a very uncooperative dog I fled from the auditorium to the sanctuary of my cottage.'

'We both dealt with her outrageous behaviour in the same way', Jean said.

'Yes, and the village deals with her by ignoring her when she's officious.'

Jean nodded her approval of the Setright containment strategy and changed the subject.

'So, you were a public servant.'

She put me on the spot. I could hardly deny that I'd been a public servant because I was the one who'd spread the rumour and I still didn't want anyone in the village to know that I'd been a policeman.

'Yes, I served the public,' I said. 'Take no notice of the Setright view of public servants.' But it was my turn to change the subject. 'This is excellent Madeira cake,' I added after I'd swallowed the last of my slice. 'Did you make it yourself?'

'Yes, and not from a packet either. I used to cook for shearers. You had to know how to cook to cook for shearers.'

'You were a shearers' cook?' was my incredulous response as I compared her elegance and charm and careful grooming with the pale flatulence and lack of any regard for personal hygiene associated with my perception of a shearers' cook.

'Joe, my husband, had a sheep farm in the Goulburn valley north of Melbourne. It was a small operation as far as sheep stations go and we didn't need, nor could we afford, a full shearing team. We engaged four shearers and a wool presser and Joe filled in with the other jobs. He looked after the machinery, kept the tally and worked as a general rouseabout while I did the cooking.'

'You were the boss lady helping out with the cooking,' I said happy to have resolved what would have been an obvious misreading of her status, but I don't think she was happy to be called the boss lady.

'It wasn't just the cooking I helped out with. We had no children and I worked beside Joe every day. We had to keep the farm viable.'

I wondered what had happened to Joe. I assumed that he'd died, but I didn't want to ask her directly.

'It's devastating when a partner whose been part of you for most of your life's journey dies and you have to travel on alone to the end, particularly when your partner is there one day and gone the next. My wife died in a car accident.'

She expressed her deep sympathy and said that she knew the burden that I carried and then she said something I wasn't expecting.

'My burden was different, though. Joe wasn't dead, he was still there.'

I was confused. I didn't know whether they'd separated or whether she was one of those people who compensate for the death of a partner by continuing to have conversations with him as she involved him in her daily life.

'You left Joe in Queenscliff,' I said to cover both speculations in my response.

'Oh no,' she said. 'Joe died after two years. I'd better explain.'

'There's no need to if it's painful for you. I meant it when I said that I had no need to intrude on your privacy.'

'I have a need to talk about it, here in my own home that is, not in the cold anonymity of an auditorium.'

'You'll find me a good listener then,' I replied and she told her story.

'When Joe retired, we sold the farm and moved to Queenscliff to live in the fisherman's cottage we'd acquired there as a weekender. We had enough money now to buy our live-aboard cruiser, a 1990 Mustang, wide body, 32-foot model with a comfortable sleeping cabin and a galley to dream about to augment the generously appointed fishing deck. For one full year we fished Port Phillip Bay for Salmon, Flathead, Trevally, and Whiting and we ventured out into the ocean swells of Bass Strait to chase the Snapper and more of the Salmon.

'We knew every pier from Williamstown down to Queenscliff and from Mordialloc to Sorrento on the other side, as we went ashore to discover what the towns and villages had to offer. It was a year like no other completely given over to recreation and pleasure giving no warning of the sudden termination of all our happiness together. Joe suffered a massive stroke that robbed him of any ability to communicate and he lingered on in that state for two long years. I felt like a bride jilted on her honeymoon. Joe had gone and he left me nursing a complete stranger.'

I didn't know what to say. The tragedy suffered by another human being can stir you with compelling empathy, but words to express your feeling don't come easily. When Nerida was killed, she went instantly and didn't feel any pain or have to struggle with a chronic disability that sapped all happiness. It would be trite for me to say that I knew how Jean felt caring for her unresponsive husband for two years.

'You have woken from a nightmare,' I said. 'I hope your happy years with Joe will enrich the new life you are seeking here at Serendipity.'

'I often talked to Joe about Brisbane,' she replied. 'He'd never been to Brisbane, but I lived here for three years during the war before I met him. I know he'd understand why I've decided to end my days here.'

She didn't expand on her decision to come and I had no intention of intruding any further on her past. I talked about Serendipity's capacity to satisfy diverse needs and avoided its capacity to hurt and reject newcomers. I also avoided asking her about any interests she might have beyond fishing and failed to discover an interest we had in common. I left her though that morning happy that I had established a genuine friendship with my new neighbour.

Chapter 4

I asked Jean if she'd like to drop in on the next ukulele practice and give me an honest opinion on how we sounded. You can't tell what sort of noise fills the auditorium when you are playing the ukulele in the middle of a group that may or may not be hitting the right chords or sustaining the right rhythm or whose off-key vocals are by no means harmonious. Jean protested that she herself was tonally challenged, but I reminded her that she liked listening to music and all I wanted her to do was to say whether what we were playing could be classified as music.

She seemed pleased then to be offered the role of music critic no matter how basic the role was because she said that when she sang out of tune, she knew she was out of tune so there was nothing wrong with her ear for music only with her ability to produce the right note on demand.

Unfortunately, she couldn't make it to our next practice because on that day her nephew was arriving from Melbourne and she had to drive to the airport to pick him up.

I met Barnaby Reid, Jean's nephew, soon after he arrived at Serendipity. He was a typical Reid, Jean had said, well built, sandy complexion with receding hair and eyes that took up the challenge of communicating with people given the tendency of lips to remain firmly closed whenever possible, and I now recognised the validity of her description of him.

'So, Barnaby,' I said 'you've come to see that your aunt is well settled in.' Jean answered for him.

'There's no need for him to settle me in. Barnaby has another talent that I'm taking advantage of.'

'We'd better get things rolling then,' Barnaby said breaking his silence.

Jean apologised for having to rush off, but assured me that it was necessary for her to go and equally necessary for the secrecy of their mission to be maintained.

I didn't see much of her for a full week, but I didn't begrudge her the time she was spending with her nephew. I had the feeling that he had a problem. Perhaps he was autistic and needed the therapy of his aunt's full attention. Whatever it was I had no wish to be privy to any of her family secrets. I have to admit that not knowing everything about a person's background and motivation is more stimulating for me than complete predictability in people. Unlike most of the people in this village for example, I'm not attracted to people like Elvira and Julius Monkton. The Monkton's are the sort of people who like to promote themselves and they take every opportunity to broadcast their opinions and their lifestyle that they assume is of vital interest to the community at large. They are due back from their holiday next Wednesday. They've been away for a month and it seems that every one in the village is looking forward to their home coming and the slide show they'll present in the auditorium to give their holiday a second lease of life. I won't be taking the trouble to participate vicariously in any holiday that they've chosen. I'll stay well away unless of course Jean wants to go. I'll put up with all sorts of inconvenience to be able to stroll down to the auditorium with Jean and sit beside her while the Monkton slide show runs its course.

To the horror of most of the Village, however, the slides of the Monkton 1995 holiday were never projected onto the screen because the Monktons no longer had their screen or their state-of-the-art projector. They had gone with their computer and printer, and all the Stirling silverware that used to be displayed in their three-bedroom cottage. But that was not the worst of it. Their walls had been left stark and comfortless or for the Monktons they were left devoid of due pomp and circumstance without the Hugh Sawreys and Margaret Olleys and the Patricia Cummings oils and the one Homer Winslow, and the cherished Henry Raeburn that was their pride and joy. Everything of value had been spirited away in the one massive heist. It was a catastrophe for a Retirement Village that topped an impressive list of Village features with the promise of absolute security behind high walls and locked gates.

I stayed well away from the house that had managed to get itself burgled against all odds. I'd conducted too many such investigations to be curious about what was going on. Residents who did go to 122 Rosella Lane to have a look wouldn't get any further than the constable on guard outside while the forensic people inside dusted for finger prints and searched for clues.

I knew how they'd be feeling, frustrated at this stage because the crims who had penetrated the security of Serendipity were professionals, and they wouldn't be leaving any calling cards.

Rachael Parker, our Village manager, was a manager who worked tirelessly to balance the expectations of residents for perfection against the need for the Village owners to profit from their investment, but the break-in shone the spotlight directly on herself and she knew it as I discovered in the course of a casual conversation with her. She was preoccupied with self-examination. Was there some flaw or laxity in her management of keys? Could she have done more to keep the cottages under supervision while their owners were away? Was there some way in which she could involve all residents in the internal security of the village?

She must have decided that all of us could be involved in the investigation of the crime because a few days later she called a meeting of all residents to be addressed by the police inspector in charge of investigating break-ins. I went along to the meeting with Jean, but as soon as I walked through the door, I wished I hadn't come. I knew the policeman who was there to talk to us. It was Chief Inspector Gil Rankin who'd come to Rockhampton as a raw young policeman and had rapidly hit the promotion trail. I directed June to a seat at the back of the gathering and tried my best the be anonymous.

Gil Rankin spoke of the spate of break-ins around the country that had been specifically targeted to reap a rich harvest and that had been so well planned and executed that no arrests had been possible and it looked as though the Serendipity heist was another such case. However, he said that Serendipity offered hope for a breakthrough because the location of the crime was different. Not only was it securely locked against outsiders, but it included at least 150 people inside the gates any one of whom may have seen something unusual afoot during the period from Monday 4th September to Wednesday 4th October when the house in Rosella Lane was unoccupied, or someone may have seen something since then, an unusual vehicle in the village or a change in the behaviour of a neighbour. He requested that we keep our eyes open and report anything that could be relevant by ringing the number on the Flyer that would be put in everyone's letter box. He undertook to extract any meat from the observations that came from us.

I thought he was making a rod for his own back soliciting an unlimited pile of potentially useless information, but when he added that any call, we made would be confidential and the neighbour across the road would never find out who reported on him, I was alarmed. I had visions of neighbour spying on neighbour and dobbing each other in for coming home late or carrying over large parcels or whatever activity they took exception to. I was so alarmed about the erosion of our privacy that I was about to risk unmasking myself by raising an objection to the open and unlimited nature of the request he'd made. Our Village manager, however, stepped in and with commendable diplomacy saved me the huge inconvenience of blowing my cover.

'Thank you, Chief Inspector Rankin,' she said. 'I can assure you that the Village will do everything it can to assist you in the investigation, but permit me to add a few caveats to your request to the residents to ring you. I want residents to act responsibly and ring, but I ask you all not to discuss your call with any resident other than your partner before or after you ring. Don't be guilty of starting any rumours about anyone in the Village. I don't want Serendipity Village to become a sort of ghetto where neighbour spies on neighbour. Secondly if you are genuinely concerned about something you've seen, but don't want to get involved, come to me and talk about it. If it doesn't relate to something I've authorized, I will ring the Inspector for you and without reference to you. Thirdly, you may not want to get involved because you don't want to incriminate yourself.'

'You think one of us did it, Rachael?' someone called out.

'No, I don't, but you may realize now that something you did or said may have inadvertently assisted the criminals to carry out the robbery. For example, you may have been talking about the village to a stranger and satisfied the stranger's curiosity about who was going on holidays. If you now realize that you've said too much, tell me about it and I will save you the embarrassment of identifying yourself to the police.'

Chief Inspector Rankin acknowledged the wisdom of Rachael's suggestions, but he added that he needed to get information and whether it came directly to him or through the Village manager it would be no less useful.

'Let's go,' I said to Jean as soon as he'd finished talking. We slipped away as everyone else was standing up and forming themselves into little discussion huddles all over the room. I left her at her place no doubt to download the highlights of the meeting to Barnaby while I entered my unit through my back door, relieved that I'd escaped the notice of Gil Rankin.

I should have known better. DCI Rankin didn't rise in the service because he didn't notice things. He was knocking on my door an hour after the meeting just as I was about to sit down to my lunch.

'Surprise, surprise,' he said when I opened the door.

'Gil Rankin,' I said. 'You spotted me at the meeting.'

'Yes, I was looking out for you.'

'You'd better come in,' I said, glancing up the lane. 'You knew I was here?'

'Not until I saw your name on the list of residents. I asked Rachael Parker if she had any retired police inspectors at the Village and she assured me that she didn't.'

'I'd like to keep it that way,' I said.

'I understand that, but I want to put a proposition to you.'

'Could you do with a cup of tea and a sandwich?' I said.

'Why not, it's right on lunch time,' he replied.

I boiled the jug again and made four more ham and tomato sandwiches. When we were sitting at the table, he put his proposition. He wanted me to accept a short-term contract to investigate the crime that had been committed in my village.

I declined of course. I'd retired from the Police Force and I'd settled in to a very different life.

'No, no,' he said. 'I'm not asking you to abandon your new life. You have the perfect cover to observe the life of the Village without alerting anyone to what it is you are really dong. You must continue to be the uninspiring, low-grade, desk-bound retired public servant that you've established as your persona.'

'You've been checking up on me and drawing attention to me. I didn't want to be seen as someone of interest to the police.'

'That's the last thing I'd do to someone I hoped would be working undercover in a retirement village. I was checking the Residents' list in Rachael Parker's office and I came across Frank Coleman. I said that I knew a Frank Coleman who was a Police Inspector when he retired and I asked her if there were any retired Police Inspectors at Serendipity. She smiled and said that the Frank Coleman at Serendipity was never in the police force and certainly not inspector material. He was just a low-grade, desk-bound uninspiring public servant.'

I was happy to hear myself so described and I began to warm to the idea of investigating a crime without stepping away from the comfort of that assumed role. I said as much to Gil stressing the necessity that no one at the Village was to know that I'd been a police officer.

'There'll have to be a partial stepping away from your assumed role,' he said.

'I don't think so,' I said. 'I'm either under cover or not under cover and I can't help you if I'm not under complete cover.'

'Your undercover role will run more smoothly if the Village manager is able to sanction whatever it is, you'll need to do in the Village. She's a very intelligent woman. You'll find her easy to work with as I have done.'

'You've already recruited her as an honorary sheriff!'

'I thought it might have been obvious. We played a sort of good cop bad cop game in our presentation to the meeting. I didn't want any dobbing in to get out of hand.'

'Thank goodness for that. I thought you were ignoring the wellbeing of the village in a dubious attempt to get what you wanted. I was about to protest until Rachael took over, but you are still going to be inundated with useless calls from Serendipity. You might have been better off diverting the calls to Crime Stoppers.'

'Crime Stopper calls are non-urgent and there's a definite policy not to record them to protect the callers. There's no need to worry though about me being inundated. I'll be recording them all and passing them on to you if you are going to be on my staff. With your knowledge of the residents, you won't have any trouble sorting out the stirrers from the ones that have useable information.'

I kept to myself the thought that he didn't want to get me back into the force for my detection skills, but to deal with the phone calls from Serendipity. We kept talking on over a long lunch and he left happy that I'd agreed to join his staff for the duration of the investigation.

Chapter 5

There was no need for me to wait for the official document signed by the Police Commissioner contracting my services as a police officer to investigate the break-in at Serendipity. I commenced work as soon as Chief Inspector Rankin left. Not that anyone would have noticed. All the residents would see was Frank Coleman wandering around looking as though he was lost.

Gil Rankin told me that the Forensic team had drawn a blank inside 122 Rosella Lane so there was no need for me to try to inveigle my way in to the house to carry out clandestine investigations. The stolen goods were now either hidden in the village or they'd been removed from the village and were by now well away from the village precinct. In either case it's possible that the burglars may have left a foot print of the operation somewhere along the route they took to try to secure their ill-gotten gains.

It didn't seem likely to me that the contents of 122 Rosella Lane lay hidden in the village. All the buildings other than the cottages were public places or places that could be easily checked. The Administration Office, the Auditorium, the Library and Games room, the Craft room, the Change rooms for the swimming pool, the Restaurant, and the three Neighbour

Centres gave no opportunity for covert storage and I'll suggest that Rachael checks the Maintenance shed and the Garden shed as part of her normal responsibility to keep an eye on all Village property and equipment.

That leaves the cottages. I'll acquire the master key and check the twelve cottages that are currently empty waiting for buyers, but I'll have to recommend to Gil Rankin that he organizes a search of all the occupied cottages. He won't like doing it because it will become civil liberties headlines, but even the outside chance that some spare bedroom has been turned into a thieves' kitchen makes a search necessary. If a member of the Serendipity staff like Rachael herself or the Sales Officer or the Village Nurse accompanies the police officer to protect the rights of the resident it might be seen by the residents as right and proper to cooperate.

However they react won't be my worry. I'll probably object myself when they come to search my place to distance myself from the police who think it's their right to trash your privacy, but I'll be concentrating on my segment of the investigation with the same conviction that the police have a right to intrude if it's suspected that a crime has been committed.

I sat down on one of the garden seats provided in the Village for octogenarian walkers and pictured in my mind the thieves entering and exiting by the main gate or through one of the doors in the eastern wall and once outside, loading a waiting van with the loot. I needed to know which exit they would have used to give my investigation a firm starting point. Would they have used the door in the wall closest to 122 Rosella Lane or the exit that gave the best escape route once they were outside? I took out my note book and biro and sketched a map of the village and its surrounds.

Serendipity is adjacent to Gympie Road but there is no access to it from the busy highway. The main gate gives entry from Aspley Road through the southern wall. The northern wall has no gate or door because our northern neighbour is a service station and behind the service station is a fenced in mobile phone tower. A lane runs between the service station and the Serendipity wall to give Telstra vehicles access to the tower.

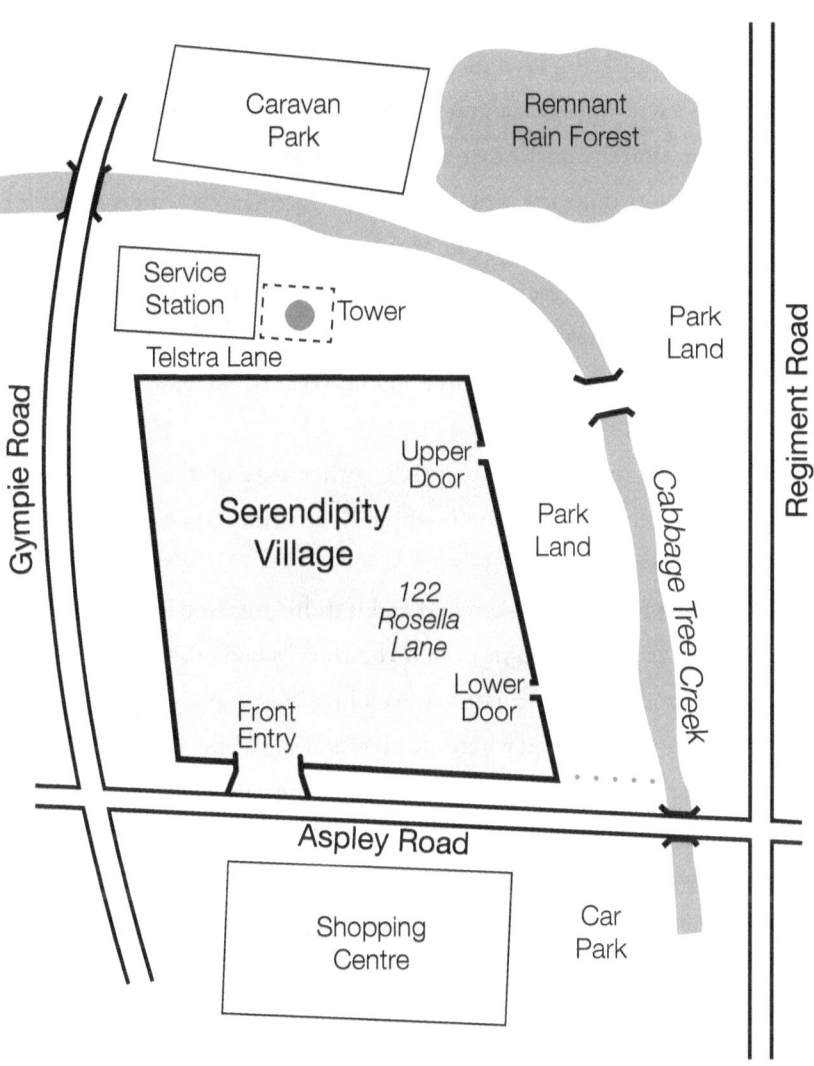

Map of Serendipity Village
and its surrounds

The eastern wall has two doors that open on to parkland between Serendipity and Cabbage Tree Creek. The creek runs parallel to the eastern wall and then bends around past the northern side of the service station and then under the bridge on Gympie Road.

There is a walking track along the creek bank that crosses the creek via a bridge just beyond the north-east corner of the village.

Which way would the thieves want to go once they were outside? I sketched in features beyond the immediate surrounds of the village. Across Aspley Road facing the main gate, there is a Supermarket surrounded by its car park and across Cabbage Tree creek to the east I sketched in another stretch of park land bordered by Regiment Road to the east and a patch of remnant rainforest to the north.

Beyond the service station on the other side of the creek there's a Caravan Park with its entry from Gympie Road. The Caravan Park stretches right back to the rainforest.

I looked at the map I'd sketched and it didn't take me long to eliminate the main gate as the exit point even if the thieves had managed to get hold of a key card to open it. The gate was well lit all night and in full view of the supermarket across the road where cleaners and shelf fillers would be coming and going and the cleaner responsible for the car park could spend most of the night noticing what was going on outside Serendipity.

122 Rosella Lane was closest to the lower gate in the East wall, but the drawback for any thief getting away from the crime scene through it was the light from Aspley Road that filtered into that part of the park particularly if he had to get to his car parked outside the bollards that denied cars entry to the park from Aspley Road. However, no well-informed thief would have chosen the lower door because there is a barking dog in the lane leading up to it.

The only exit that suits the needs of a clandestine departure from Serendipity in the middle of the night is the upper door in the eastern wall that gives access to an unlit parkland and to which a vehicle can be driven unobserved down the lane past a service station that switches out its lights at 7pm.

It did not escape my notice too that a vehicle can also cross the foot bridge over Cabbage Tree Creek that's been built wide enough to carry a tractor and mowing equipment to service both sections of the park. The thief or thieves could leave that doorway and drive right through to Regiment Road untroubled by any fence or unwelcome light from the dark road.

Satisfied that I'd picked the right exit point I set about examining the doorway precinct both inside and outside the Village. It may have been weeks since the break-in and I didn't expect to find anything given the amount of traffic that had passed that way including the Serendipity walkers on their monthly excursion to locations beyond the village. But I examined the ground carefully anyway.

Less used, probably, was the laneway to the Telstra Tower and I was able to distinguish a couple of unusual tyre tracks in the light gravel roadway. I took photographs of them to pass on to the Forensic team who would determine if they'd been made by Telstra vehicles or a vehicle with less right to be in the lane.

As I walked back, I spotted Jean and Barnaby on the bridge over Cabbage Tree Creek. Barnaby was striding along carrying what looked like a full knapsack on his back and Jean seemed to be hurrying to keep up with him. I waited for them to reach me.

'Pleasant afternoon for a walk,' I said as they approached.

'We do what we have to do, pleasant or unpleasant,' Jean replied.

Barnaby didn't say anything, He seemed keen to keep going to charge through the gate ahead of us.

'Don't think Barnaby rude, it's just his way,' Jean said.

'No, no I don't think he's rude. I think you are doing an excellent job going on these walks with him.'

I actually thought that he could be acrophobic and Jean was trying some open space therapy with him, He seemed to be cooperating because he was keen to get going on that first day, but he's also very keen to get back home. Jean obviously wasn't keen to talk about it so I changed the subject to the robbery.

'I wonder how many residents will ring the police with information about who did it,' I said.

'Most of them will know who did it, but they all can't be right. I know Martha Setright will get it wrong.'

'Who will she nominate?'

'Me of course. She thinks I tried to hide where I came from so there's something dodgy about me. Elvira and Julius Monkton were robbed soon after I arrived on the scene. What further evidence does she need?'

'Fortunately for you the police will be looking for evidence that will stand up in court. They won't take any notice of Martha Setright.'

We continued our chatting until we reached Jean's place. I left her to the silence of Barnaby and continued onto my own cottage. I entered through the back door and went straight out through the front door to wind my way through the village to the Administration Office.

Gil Rankin had determined that he would relay any messages for me through Rachael Parker and if, possible, I was to call in on her at 4.45 pm each day. I was to enter her office through her back door which was hidden from view by a large hibiscus bush. I approved of the precaution. I wanted no speculation about a down at heel former public servant hanging around the front office to visit the village manager. Glancing around to ensure that I wasn't being observed, I knocked on her door with a lively anticipation about my meeting with her as an undercover policeman.

Chapter 6

'Frank Coleman', Rachael Parker said when she opened the back door to let me into her office, 'I owe you an apology', she added when I was seated.

'Why'? I said.

'Because I assured Inspector Rankin that you were never a policeman and definitely not inspector material. I'm sorry, I called you a low-grade public servant.'

'You are to be congratulated because you didn't treat me as less equal despite your lowly opinion of my working life which, I might add, was the working life I circulated soon after I came here.'

'We treat everyone with the same regard at Serendipity no matter what they were before they retired. Unfortunately many of the residents aren't prepared to be so inclusive. I'm worried that some of them will be drawing all sorts of perverse conclusions about what their neighbours are doing when they talk to Chief Inspector Rankin.'

'I suspect that that is the main reason why Gil Rankin has resurrected me from a slumbering retirement. He needed someone who knew the village to sort out the wheat from the chaff. To retain the strict confidentiality of the calls, it had to be a serving policeman.'

'He is concerned about confidentiality. He left the first cassette with me to pass on to you, but he checked our letter boxes and found that the packet would slip through the slot, so all future cassettes will be mailed directly to you. He recognized that my office secretary could be opening packages that arrived and leaving them in my in-tray. He didn't want stories getting round that I was regularly receiving confidential cassettes.'

'Good I'm glad that's sorted out. If my dropping in on you on a regular basis was picked up by a gossip, it would be just as damaging to your reputation as receiving confidential, cassettes. There's another issue, however, that I want to float with you. Have you thought of the implications if the robbery was an inside job and the stolen goods are still hidden in the village?'

'That had crossed my mind,' she replied, 'I've already done a stock take in the two sheds and I've checked the empty cottages. It's the ones that are waiting for refurbishment that needed to be checked. There's no possibility of hiding anything in a cottage that is currently being refurbished and once they are refurbished, prospective buyers are inspecting them with the sales officer or with me. Nothing would stay hidden for long.'

'What about the occupied cottages? How can we be sure that there's no locked spare bedroom somewhere full of Monkton possessions awaiting their final relocation?'

Rachael was silent as she contemplated a response to my question. When it came her answer demonstrated that the question had more than crossed her mind.

'I'm afraid that we can't be sure that the stolen goods are not hidden in the village. Serendipity guarantees all residents that no one can get through the door of a cottage legally unless they are invited in by the owner of the cottage and that includes me and any policeman without a search warrant. I have good legal advice that the court will not issue a search warrant for police to conduct a general search of all cottages in a village. The police would have to present firm evidence that stolen goods might be in a particular cottage to be given a warrant to search that one cottage.'

'You've done well,' I said. 'You've consulted your Serendipity solicitor.'

'It's not every day that we're broken into. I needed to know how far the police could go in their investigation.'

'Nevertheless, I have an idea how we might eliminate all the residents here from our enquiries. Do you think you could agree to accompany a police officer in a series of house inspections?'

'No, I certainly wouldn't agree! I thought I made it clear that I had to be invited in by the resident. I certainly wouldn't be inviting myself in with a police officer in tow.'

'That's understood, but you'd have no objection to helping the police with the investigation if the residents agreed to a search taking place?'

'Such an agreement is highly unlikely. I know this village, but if the police did manage to sweet talk their way in, I'd feel it my duty to be there to look after the interests of the residents.'

I laughed. 'You sound anti-police.'

'I'm not. It's you who seem to be suggesting that the police take the law into their own hands. I'm pro law and the law guarantees people privacy in their own homes if there is no evidence of anything illegal having taken place there.'

'I can assure you that the police respect that privacy, but I have an idea that might generate the cooperation of the residents in a police search. I can't tell you what it is yet because I'll have to get Gill Rankin's approval. After all he'll have to implement it. I can't, I'm under cover.

'I can't imagine what you have in mind. I hope Chief Inspector Rankin does take it up so I can find out.'

'It's nothing remarkable, just a normal police operation carried out with the cooperation of the residents. What I expect to find remarkable though are the suspicions about their neighbours that the residents have on that cassette.'

'Oh yes, the Cassette. I don't suppose I'll get to hear any of the phone calls', she said as she handed it to me.

'No you won't. Phone calls to the police are strictly confidential,'

'Typical', she said. 'You expect complete cooperation from me, but you block me out of something that might be useful to me in my job here.'

She was smiling when she said it and I knew she understood the need for police protocol in the matter of phone calls.

'You won't be blocked out' I said. 'You know everything about this village and I don't. For example, Forensics have concluded that the burglar entered No 122 using a key and it wasn't either of the house keys that the Monktons had because they took theirs with them on their holiday. What other keys do you hold in the office?'

'Only the master key that opens all the cottages and we only have two of those.'

'How secure are they?'

'They are kept locked in that key cupboard,' she said pointing to the small wall locker behind her desk, 'and only five staff members are authorised to use them after signing a register.'

'What are they used for?'

'Only to open doors for residents who have locked their keys inside their houses.'

'Are master keys ever given to residents to open their own doors?'

No, only the staff members who are authorised to use them can take them from the office.'

'Nevertheless, Rachael, I want you to get those staff members together to see if they can come up with an occasion when the master key actually left their hands. It would only take a second for someone to press a wax impression that would enable a tool maker to fashion another key.'

'Oh no, I thought our procedure with the key made it secure. We'll go through the register and try to recall what happened every time a master key was used.'

'Good', I said. 'I'll leave the staff to you while I go and listen to the phone calls.'

Back at my cottage I retrieved my regulation police cassette player from a box in the bottom of my wardrobe. I pressed in the cassette and settled back on my bed on a stack of pillows to listen.

The first caller introduced herself as Mavis Shand. I knew her, not well, but I'd often admired her garden. She was one of those residents who'd opted to look after her own patch of garden and she planted it with some exotic and colourful plants that not only produced a brilliant spring display but she also managed to have something in bloom throughout the year.

Given her love of gardening, I was totally unprepared for the man she named as responsible for the theft at No 122. It was Tom Greenveld the Gardener, and she said she'd almost caught him red handed. Late one afternoon during the time the Monktons were away she had spotted him on the roof of No 122. She thought at the time that a gardener had no right to be up on a roof, but when the break-in was discovered, she knew immediately what he'd been doing up there. He was getting the skylight open to give himself a noiseless access to the cottage during the night. She painted Tom Greenveld as a moral delinquent whom she'd never trusted and she was 99 % certain that he was the man the police needed to question over the break-in at 122 Rosella Lane.

I thought about Mavis Shand's certainty and decided I would have to give each suspect a score out of ten with 10 indicating a complete certainty of my own. Mavis Shand's evidence was only circumstantial. Tom Greenveld was on the roof, but a man can climb up on a roof for all sorts of legitimate reasons. However, Mavis' firm conviction that he was guilty seemed to have an echo in the doubt that Rachael must have had when she searched the garden shed. I would want the shed searched because it's police procedure to assume that everyone is guilty until investigation allows them to be struck off the list of suspects. Rachael though isn't a police woman. She must have had some real concern about Greenveld to go straight to that shed and conduct that search.

I dialled the number Rachael had given me and when she answered I said, 'Is your number secure?'

'Yes, Frank, it is,' she replied with no hesitation about placing my voice. 'I've given you my direct number, it's not switched through from the outer office.'

'Good, yes, it is Frank here. 'I'm ringing to ask you about your gardener. He's been accused of the crime by a caller. Did you also suspect him when you decided to search his shed?'

'Of course not, Tom Greenveld has been a trusted staff member for ten years.'

'Why search his shed?'

'Because I needed to search the maintenance shed. Mark Dollinger has been here less than a year. I didn't want him thinking I was looking for stolen goods there so I did a stock take in both places.'

'You are very diplomatic. Are you too diplomatic to ask Tom Greenveld what he was doing on the roof of 122 Rosella Lane while the Monktons were away?'

'I don't have to ask him. He was up there cleaning out the gutters. There's a Silky Oak near the house that clogs the gutters when it drops its flowers. Before he left, Julius Monkton reminded me that the gutters needed to be cleaned before the summer rains started. Gutters are usually looked after by maintenance, but when he's snowed under, I use the gardener.'

'Well that evaporates most of the evidence against him. He can hardly be a suspect if his boss gives him an impeccable character reference and she's also responsible for him being on the roof.'

'I notice you are being careful to avoid telling me who accused him,' Rachael said.

'Yes, it's against police protocol to disclose police sources.'

'It's not against any protocol for me to tell you who made the complaint. It was Mavis Shand, wasn't it?'

'Seeing you know I can hardly deny it. I suppose there's a story behind her nastiness.'

'Yes, there is. I didn't realize the business was still so raw. A couple of years ago Mavis included some colourful little lantana shrubs in her display. Tom told her they were noxious weeds an she'd have to pull them out. She refused and Tom came to me and I put a letter together, but I contacted the village owners and suggested that the letter should come from them to guard against an escalating dispute within the village. The owners were happy to oblige and Mavis was offered replacement plants if the lantana was removed before the end of the month. If they weren't removed by the deadline, the gardener would be instructed to pull them out and destroy them. Tom ended up pulling them out and she's never forgiven him.'

'What is it with people that they allow a minor incident to grow into a major row?' I said.

'Mavis wouldn't regard interference with her garden as something minor, but she does have to get over it. I need to talk to her.'

'You can't do that. You're not supposed to know that she rang the police to accuse him of larceny. She was promised that her call would be confidential.'

Of course. I wouldn't dream, of upsetting your protocol.'

'I thanked her for her help and ended the call. She'd put paid to any prospect of Tom Greenveld getting on my list of suspects.

The next caller on the police tape was Ray Gasper. I wasn't surprised because he was the sort of person who always had something to say. He was a loudmouth and his jarring voice did its best to dominate any meeting or social gathering that he was part of. For that reason, Ray wasn't well liked. His wife Jane, however, was everyone's favourite person. Her voice was soothing and she was sensitive to the feelings of others and by thinking before she spoke, she always had something positive to say. I'd got to know her because she was in the ukulele group. I admired the precision of her fingering which always delivered perfect chords, and the rhythm of her strumming that effortlessly adapted to the needs of the vocals.

With a mind-set that had the dispositions of husband and wife firmly fixed, it took me a few moments to realize that Ray Gasper was not coming through true to form. He was speaking quietly and he was selecting phrases carefully to underline his confidence in the integrity of his fellow residents and suggesting that the police should concentrate their search for the perpetrators of the break-in in the caravan park across the creek where the itinerant population was less stable. I was convinced that he was talking to a script prepared by his wife Jane. Left to his own ubiquitous spontaneity he would be stridently condemning the caravan park as a hot bed of rowdy scumbags and intransigent felons who belonged in jail and needed to be locked up without wasting time on the assumption of innocence.

Such ranting cannot be taken seriously, but the quiet reference to instability at the caravan park prompted the note I wrote in my case book. 'Check that Gil has got hold of caravan park registrations between September 4 and October 4.

The third and last call on the tape was the one that Jean predicted. Martha Setright was banging on about her sister, who lives on the Gold Coast, telling her about all the break-ins on the coast a while back. They ceased there about a week before Jean Reid arrived at Serendipity from just over the border. It didn't take any stretch of Martha's imagination to establish a connection with the burglary at 122 particularly when a young man arrived and they went off together, with him carrying a knapsack on his back. She'd been watching Jean Reid and it didn't escape her attention that she'd formed a liaison with Frank Coleman another resident who thinks it's OK to ignore the rules for living that society establishes to civilize itself.

I thought of Roger Masters again and his little talk about conventional wisdom that he said was made up of all those ideas that are passed down through the generations and that people accepted with no thought given to them at all.

Roger said that it was conventional wisdom that stopped people growing up and thinking for themselves as adults. I didn't fully appreciate what he was saying at the time, but Martha Setright came through now as a clear example of what he meant.

'You need to join our philosophy club', was the only comment I made on her contribution to the investigation.

Chapter 7

G il Rankin took up, with some enthusiasm, my germ of an idea to get the village cooperation in allowing a police search of all the cottages and he contacted the Police Academy to work out the modus operandi with one of the lecturers. A graduating class of twenty cadets were to be given a practical exercise in looking for real evidence that real stolen goods were hidden in real homes after a robbery had really taken place in a real neighbourhood. The neighbourhood was to be, of course, Serendipity Retirement Village. The students were to study and make themselves familiar with the items taken from 122 Rosella Lane, but to cover the likely eventuality that no stolen goods would be found, a silver goblet was to be placed in each of twenty of the cottages so that each of the twenty students would have the opportunity to find a substitute stolen item.

There are 150 cottages at Serendipity so each of the students would be assigned seven or eight cottages to search and maps of the village were prepared with the search area for each student highlighted. Also prepared were report forms for the residents who would be assessing the cadets.

Gil couldn't help being pleased with the operation that had been worked out by the Academy and with the work that they had already done to ensure that it would run smoothly and he expected me to be pleased too, but there was an obvious floor in the plan.

'Gil,' I said, 'what about permission to enter the cottages? The police cadets can't go into any cottage unless they get permission. You know that.'

Gil continued to smile. 'Taken care of,' he said.

'You can't take care of an issue like that. Only the occupier can give permission to enter and you haven't even called a meeting of the residents yet.'

'The Academy suggested how it might be done and that's why they've gone ahead with all the preparations. They lobbied the village manager with a request that Serendipity Village participates in an exercise to provide Academy students with a practical learning experience, one that involved communicating with the public and searching a house for stolen goods without unduly upsetting the people in the house. To avoid attracting Media attention at this stage it was suggested that there be no village advertisement for volunteers but a quiet selection of twenty participants by the Manager herself. The twenty participants would give each cadet one cottage to search and the stolen item they'd be searching for would be a silver goblet hidden in each of the cottages. Twenty goblets from the Academy dining room would be made available for the exercise.'

'You're not telling me that Rachael Parker accepted the request as a genuine project to help the Police Academy?'

'Of course she didn't. She rang to tell me that the letter she got sounded like a cunning scheme to get the police into the cottages to search for real stolen goods. I admitted that you and I were involved, but at the same time I pointed out that it would be excellent publicity for Serendipity when it was finally reported. Serendipity would be known as the village where the older generation cooperates in the training of young policemen to carry out their duties less officiously and more tuned to the need to respect the rights of people in the community.'

'Good publicity was the right button to press to get Rachael Parker to rise to the challenge,' I said.

'Yes, it was, and she had no trouble getting twenty residents ready and willing to participate. All that remains now is to address a meeting of all residents and tell them about the project and persuade everyone not involved to get involved by nominating their cottages to be added to the twenty already participating.

I must admit that I was impressed with the development of my idea. I went to the residents' meeting that was duly called and sat with Jean at the back of the room, not to hide from Gil Rankin this time, but to keep my fellow residents under observation.

Rachael thanked us all for coming and handed the meeting over to the Chief Inspector. Gil started off by thanking the Village for all the phone calls, all of which, he said, gave useful leads that the police were following up with due diligence. That's one way of putting it I thought. There were twelve phone calls in all but for most of them no diligence at all was due. Tom Greenveld, the gardener, was not a suspect, nor was Jean Reid or her nephew, or me for that matter. Subsequent calls that were motivated by irrational prejudice like the one that tried to implicate Roger Masters because he'd been heard questioning the existence of God needed no follow up investigation. Neither did the one that pushed a particular circumstance to the limit to suggest that a crime was underway. It didn't take much to establish that the removal van parked outside No 96 for over an hour was not there to collect stolen goods, but because the driver was having lunch with his parents. As far as I was concerned there were only two calls that warranted further attention and both of them were on the police Radar already. We had the Caravan Park down as a place of interest for us and as far as the other call was concerned it was almost axiomatic that we would suspect that the theft of paintings and jewellery and other valuable artifacts may have been an attempt to defraud an insurance company. I had listened to this last call with interest because it seemed that I wasn't the only person to be turned off by the Monkton pomp and circumstance.

While these thoughts about the phone calls were occupying my mind, Gil was explaining to his audience the nature and purpose of the project that twenty Serendipity residents had signed up for and he was at the point of handing out the report forms that were to be used by the residents to evaluate the way the police Cadets went about their task. This report form was put together by the Academy and both Gil and I thought it would be the *coup de grace* in getting the cooperation we needed. The residents would not be required to write anything but simply select comments from the list of comments that matched their own feeling about aspects of the search like the way the cadets greeted residents at the door, the explanation they gave of their task, the diligence of their search and their success in leaving everything as they found it before the search.

When Gil had finished talking, he called for comments from the residents. Nobody responded and the room was as quiet as a room full of students concentrating on their examination papers. I was disappointed. Some residents would need to give their whole hearted support to the exercise to motivate others to sign up for it. If the number involved stayed at twenty, it might be a useful exercise for the Academy, but there would still be 130 residents who would not be eliminated from the suspect list. I would have to speak. After all it was my idea and I didn't want it to fail. Concluding that the silence wasn't going to be broken, I was on my feet.

'Madam Chair,' I said addressing Rachael, I for one will not be taken in by police attempts to get into my house without a search warrant. The law doesn't allow their entry so why should I invite them in on the dubious pretext that I'll be helping in their education. I' not that gullible.'

Before I sat down Martha Setright was on her feet.

'What's Frank Coleman trying to hide? If he's got nothing to hide, all I can say is that his lack of community spirit is unbelievable. Of course we are responsible for the education of the younger generation. If we want the sort of police force, we can be proud of, it's up to us to get involved in their education. I'll be signing up to play my part and all right-thinking people will do the same.

Ray Gasper spoke next and it was a Ray Gasper who had returned to his old form back from the quietly reasonable Ray of the phone call. His wife Jane was sitting beside him but this time she wasn't exercising any restraining influence over him.

'It really makes me mad as Hell when I think that the police need a Court order to go after criminals. Catching criminals is their job for God's sake and they should have been here as soon as the break-in was discovered to conduct their house-to-house search. It's pathetic that they have to ask our permission and design a search as an education exercise for their police academy. It's not their fault that they have to do that, it's ours as a community. It's high time that we stopped getting in their way. Let's all throw open our houses instead of acting like bandicoots backing down bolt holes, and let the police find out who's guilty.

It didn't surprise me when Roger Masters rejected Ray Gasper's contention that as a community we should step aside and let the police take any power they needed to do their job. I was well aware of Roger's view that we are acting like children when we accept without due consideration the power and authority of any group over us. It was a mantra for him that the only outcome of the unquestioning acceptance of authority will be the corruption of that authority and the only outcome of unchecked police power will be police corruption.

Roger was by no means a negative person and his goals for adult behaviour were well known to members of the philosophy club. They were love, justice and non-violence, goals that could not be legislated for or enforced and it will only be the long years of networking along the endless highways of the internet that will enable us to take in sufficient nourishment and finally grow up.

It didn't surprise me at all that a meeting with the agenda we had that morning didn't have time for nor would it tolerate any speaker trying to establish a philosophical thesis. Roger was cut short as soon as he mentioned the possibility of police corruption and he was followed by a range of speakers all reinforcing Martha Setright's point of view, an outcome that I intended as I stirred her to action with my negativity.

The place was a hive of activity as soon as the meeting was closed. People lined up to sign up for the house search at the three tables that were set aside for them. The police cadets trooped in from an early lunch over at the supermarket and settled themselves in chairs in one corner of the auditorium for a final pep talk from the Academy lecturer. I waited for Jean Reid and strolled home with her.

'I signed up for the search thing,' she said, 'because it doesn't suit me at the moment to stand out in the Village as someone who's different.

'Probably a sensible thing to do Jean. It's not very wise to get offside at Serendipity as I seem to have done. The only one who supported me was Roger Masters.'

'Roger Masters seems like an interesting man,' Jean said.

'He's either an interesting man or a dangerous one depending on your community perception. You should come along to the philosophy club and sort him out.

'I might do that when the current project I'm working on has been put to bed', she said.

I didn't ask what the project was and she didn't volunteer any information about it, but I thought it could have had something to do with Barnaby's problem and I understood her preference for privacy. However, her easy acceptance of and obvious pleasure in my company and my pleasure in hers and the emergence of mutual interests stirred in me a deeper longing to be always with her. Sadly for me though I was not free to entertain thoughts of a happy future together. I could only wonder if it could ever be possible that my feeling for Jean could lead to an easing of my commitment to Nerida my first wife. Nerida has been the love of my life, but there was a bond between us that could not and would not be broken by her passing. How could I give myself to another woman and keep secrets from her, particularly a secret whose telling could trash Nerida's memory and probably destroy the lives of her siblings

Chapter 8

I was sitting on my back patio confident that I wouldn't be disturbed by management with a police cadet in tow wanting to search my house, but my brain was actively engaged in getting started with my own search for the silverware and paintings stolen from 122 Rosella Lane.

I'd been keeping an ear open for any chatter that involved the Caravan Park and chatter there was aplenty because Serendipity people were very suspicious of some of the itinerants. A part of the park had been turned into a refuge for down and outs. The grey nomads swapping travellers' tales as they explored the endless variety of our big country had to share the park with spent dullards who had sunk to the bottom of the social heap where they were supported by government handouts that enabled them to occupy for regulated periods caravans that were no longer capable of touring and they supplied themselves with slabs of beer and casks of wine, analgesics for the boredom of long years of inactivity.

I waited in vain for any suggestion that someone in that caravan park might be capable of the heist at number 122. Ray Gasper was the only one who'd suggested that when he'd made his phone call to the police, but the conventional wisdom of all the gossip ruled that possibility out completely. There were criminals there of course, but their crimes were petty requiring no more cerebral stamina than was required to snatch a handbag or lift some desired item from a shop.

My thoughts didn't get beyond the general discernment that the Caravan Park lacked master criminals because Millie Mockridge and Janine Rumble from the other side of the Azalea bushes appeared on my patch of lawn.

'Millie and Janine,' I said, 'to what do I owe the pleasure of your company?'

'We thought we'd better let you know that the police cadet who visited our cottages was a charming young woman,' Millie said. 'She would have visited you too if you hadn't been so anti-police.'

'Fancy being frightened of a young woman,' Janine said.

'Hold on a minute,' I said, 'I'm not anti-police and I'm not frightened of young women. What I'm concerned about is a police force that ends up with unlimited power. Democracy takes a back seat in a police state,'

'Why do all you lefties start talking about a police state when the government is strong on law and order?' Janine said. 'If there's no law and order, it's a free for all. That's when democracy hasn't got a chance.'

'Not so long ago we had a government in this state that thought that way and who was it that ended up in Jail?' I asked.

'The police commissioner and half the cabinet,' Millie answered with no hesitation.

'Exactly, it's hardly a democracy when innocent people are being harassed and those in power take the opportunity to line their own pockets.'

'You're right ,' Millie said, 'but Janine won't agree with you. She thinks that the Fitzgerald enquiry was more damaging to the country than anything that the police ever did,'

'Of course I don't agree. Fitzgerald wrecked a strong government with his enquiry, just as Frank here tried to wreck the prospect of Serendipity Village doing its duty to help the Police Academy with its education program.'

'I did nothing to stop the house searches going ahead. I just said that I wouldn't be involved. It was a matter of principle for me that I didn't want to set aside a law that was there to protect my privacy. Nearly everyone else at the meeting saw it as an opportunity to be involved in community service and I'm happy enough about that. Everyone in a village like this should be involved in community service. There are a lot of other opportunities going begging.

'It may have escaped your notice,' Janine said, 'but people in this village are very generous with their time. They serve on the social committee; they keep the library running and they organize all sorts of activities and they raise money at our Spring Fair to provide a lot of extra facilities here.'

'You're right,' I said, 'there are no opportunities for service going begging in the Village. I was thinking of the needs outside the Village.'

Millie, however, thought that those needs were also being filled.

'A couple of years ago,' she said, 'one of our residents got a Council award for service to the whole district. He has a coffee van and he drives around serving free coffee and buns and cakes and sandwiches that he picks up from bakeries and supermarkets because they've reached their sell-by dates.'

'That was Harold Hardaker,' Janine said with a touch of contempt. His community service turned into a community disservice. People complained that whenever he stopped to serve coffee, he attracted all sorts of undesirables to his van.'

'Surely they didn't stop him serving coffee,' I said.

'No, they didn't, thank goodness,' Millie said, 'but they worked out places where he could operate where he wouldn't be annoying Janine's hoity toity friends.'

Janine started to respond when a loud knocking on my front door stopped her mid-sentence.

'You have a visitor,' Millie said. 'I'll take Janine home and deal with her there.'

'Thank you both for coming,' I said, 'and what is the name of your coffee man Millie?' I called from my back door.

'Harold Hardaker,' she called back.

I needed to talk to people who mixed with undesirables. I needed to pick up information about what the undesirables were talking about.

'Is it all over?' I said when I opened the front door and let Gill in.

'No, but there's been a development. A cadet has found an item from the Monkton house in one of the cottages. It was brought straight to me and the Monktons have confirmed that it belongs to them. I need to go and question the residents involved, but I thought I'd better get some more background on them from you first.'

'That's good news Gil. Things are starting to move, but I mightn't be able to help you with background. It's a big village and I don't know everyone in it yet.'

'You know this pair all right. It's Mrs Jean Reid and her nephew, Barnaby.'

'What! That's ridiculous. I can tell you now that whatever the cadet has reported to you, Neither Mrs Reid nor her nephew had anything to do with the robbery.'

'It's all right for you to be so confident, but I haven't retired yet. I'm a full-time policeman and I need to follow up all the evidence particularly when the pair are already suspects.'

'Suspects! They've only been accused by Martha Setright. I told you, the woman is completely deluded. She claimed in her phone call that Jean Reid was involved in Break-ins on the Gold Coast because she lived just over the border. She lived in Queenscliff down on Port Phillip Bay for God's sake. It's Kingscliff that's just over the border, and the silly woman got the two mixed up.'

'Yes, Frank, and it was you who mentioned that Jean Reid spent a year sailing Port Phillip Bay with her husband. We'll be checking to see what break-ins there were down there during that year.'

'You're going to turn this investigation into a witch hunt and you're going to stretch circumstantial evidence beyond bursting point to do it.'

'It only becomes circumstantial evidence that needs checking because she's been caught with a stolen item in her house. If it had been anyone else, you would have been in favour of following up on any lead that presented itself.'

'Well, it isn't anyone else and I'll be throwing my every effort into establishing her innocence.'

'And you have every right to do that, but I want to warn you against interfering with any actions that your colleagues in the police force see fit to take. They have every right to investigate her and if there's a case there, they'll build it up.'

'I'm confident that she's innocent. The only case that could be built up would rest on planted evidence.'

'That comment isn't worthy of a response and I'll ignore it.'

'Nevertheless you know that you can't always be 100% certain of your colleagues. That police cadet for instance, what on earth did he find and did he really find it or did he put it there?'

'It's not a he, it's a she.' She's a top cadet at the Academy and there's no way that she'd be starting her career in the force by planting evidence.'

'Oh no! Not the charming young woman who impressed my neighbours across the way. All right then, I accept that she's reliable. What was it that she found?'

'It was a pen, a biro, and the Monktons have identified it as theirs.'

I just stared at him in complete disbelief.

'Have you taken leave of your senses, Gil? Everybody has lookalike pens. They're mass produces in the millions. You really should be investigating that cadet. Didn't you ask her why she picked up a pen in that house and accused the resident of stealing it. You should be ashamed of yourself letting her charm influence your judgement like that.'

'No, I didn't ask her why she picked up the biro, and I'm not ashamed of myself, well just a little bit I suppose for stirring you up as I have. I'd better put you in the picture. She told me why she'd confiscated the pen and her conscientious approach to the job really impressed me.

All the stolen items had been photographed and listed with the insurer and she'd made herself familiar with all the markings on the silverware and all the artists represented in the Monkton collection, not just the paintings the Monktons had, all their paintings.

'The Scottish painter Henry Raeburn was one of the artists she studied. Now the pen in question was labelled *National Galleries of Scotland* and it also had printed on it ten identical figures of a man who looked as though he was skating. Our very astute young police cadet recognized the figure as the one in Henry Raeburn's painting of the Reverend Robert Walker skating on Duddingston Loch. Naturally she asked the lady of the house where the pen came from and she couldn't help noticing Barnaby's reaction. He seemed transfixed as he stared with wide eyes at his aunt. His aunt eventually said that Barnaby found it and gave it to her. Thinking that such a pen could have come from 122 Rosella Lane, she asked Barnaby exactly where he'd found it. Barnaby's consternation increased until once again his aunt supplied the answer. He found it over near the patch of remnant rainforest behind the caravan park.'

'All right,' I said, 'the cadet did very well and she's to be congratulated. Finding a pen that most likely came from the Monkton house gives us a link to the robbery that we can't ignore but, Gil, I'm asking you not to rush in to any conclusion that Jean Reid and Barnaby had anything to do with the robbery. Barnaby says that he found the pen and I believe him.'

'He'll still have to be questioned. He can't keep hiding behind his aunt. We'll need him to take us to the exact spot where he found the pen so we can extract any other clues from the area.'

'Of course, but I'm advising you that you won't get any information out of him if you go in heavy handed. He has a mental problem and he'll just clam up.'

'Thank you for pointing that out, Frank, but I'll also have to keep it in mind that you and Jean Reid seem to be developing into an item as they say and if that's the case your assessment of her can only be accepted with some reservation.'

'There you go again, Gil, making judgements on the strength of Martha Setright's phone call. There's no truth in anything that Martha Setright said. She knows nothing about either of us except that Jean and I often sit together at meetings which is only natural for neighbours who walk down to the auditorium together.'

'I don't need Martha Setright to tell me that you like the woman. I've gathered that from my conversation with you. That doesn't mean that your judgement can't be trusted but I need to put it into perspective. Thanks for your input. I'll bear it in mind as I interview them.'

He left me then and walked towards Jean's cottage at the other end of the garden. I wasn't sure how Jean was going to react to him. I knew that there were things that she held back from me. She never expanded on her reason for coming to Brisbane and she actually said that Barnaby had a talent that she was taking advantage of. Her secrets didn't bother me because I had no desire to pry into her life. Gil, though, wasn't going to accept anything but complete openness with him and he would be brutal with her until he got it. I, on the other hand, knew that I kept a secret from her. I would never talk to anyone including Jean about my life with Nerida, my first wife, so it would have been unconscionable for me to expect her to keep no secrets from me.

Chapter 9

I couldn't sit around speculating on the rugged interview that Gil would be conducting with Jean. I couldn't do anything about it. Gil was a policeman who knew how to ramp up the pressure to get to an elusive truth. The only thing I could do to protect Jean was to find that truth elsewhere.

I looked up Harold Hardaker's unit number in the Serendipity Resident's list and abandoning any thought of staging a chance meeting and a seemingly unplanned conversation with him, I was soon knocking on his door. I had no preconception of the sort of man who would open the door, but I wasn't expecting the man who did. He was tall well-built and muscular with the body of a bouncer, but with a big round face and large dreamy eyes that suggested docility and perhaps compassion. It was ,however, the sort of face that was not incompatible with pouring coffee and making sandwiches.

'I've just heard about the work you do with your coffee van,' I said without preamble as soon as he opened the door, 'and since I was passing, I thought I'd say hello and leave a small donation if you take donations.'

'Thank you,' he replied. 'The coffee van is supported by the Uniting Church and donations are welcome.'

'I was told that not everyone is happy to see coffee and buns being given away for free.'

'The recipients are certainly happy,' he said, 'but you can't please everyone. Lots of people, even some church people, don't think that homeless people and people down on their luck deserve the little bits of happiness that come their way.'

'Is it true that the council was lobbied to have the service stopped?'

'Yes, a couple of years ago, but the council came up with four locations where we could operate without causing friction. They did a good job because they nominated one location that the Church hadn't thought of.'

'Which location is that?'

Green Acres, the caravan park across the creek. Many of the church members join the grey nomads at the drop of a hat and caravanning is a life style they aspire to. People at a caravan park weren't seen as people who needed a free cup of coffee and a sandwich, but Green Acres had changed when a new management decided that there was money in cheap accommodation. Instead of replacing worn-out on-site units they moved them closer to the worn-out ablution block and rented them out cheaply. It's rumoured now that some of the cheap renters are recent releases from prison.'

Now that did interest me. Newly released prisoners often came out ready to resume a life of crime that had been organized while they were still doing time. What a perfect set-up a caravan park would provide with some grey nomad crime boss directing his criminal team without drawing attention to what he was about.

'I suppose the grey nomads and the down and outs don't mix in the park,' I said

'It' a big park and the grey nomads are well catered for down along the creek, but occasionally one of them might take an interest in what we were doing with the van. It isn't the older ones though who'll take out the social consciousness prize at Green Acres this year. It's a couple of younger men, Cody and Hank, but of course they were missionaries.'

'Missionaries!'

'Well sort of. They were Mormons and every Mormon man in America is encouraged to spend a year as a missionary in another country.'

'So two of them ended up at Green Acres helping you serve coffee and cake.'

'They did more than that. Cody and Hank weren't allowed to do any preaching at Green Acres, they did that in their own church, but they knew how to talk to ordinary people so they were popular with everyone at the caravan park. They were a breath of fresh air.

After taking me into his garage and showing me the set-up with the van, I handed him my $5 donation and congratulated him on the good work he was doing, but it was his information about ex-prisoners using the caravan park as a half-way house that interested me the most. I'd be sorting out who the ex-crims were and organizing Gil to get the reports on them that would be filed in the prison system.

I waited a couple of hours for Gil to get back to me to let me know about his interview with Jean Reid but, apparently, he'd ignored me and left the village. It didn't look good for Jean and Barnaby. I'd have to let them know that I wouldn't be leaving them to deal with intimidating police accusations by themselves. I'd be standing by them.

Jean opened the door to me and I knew at once that Gil hadn't been gentle with her. Her eyes were red and I noticed the slight tremble in her hands. Jean is a strong person and reducing her to tears would have required undue callousness on Gil's part, but I wasn't supposed to know that Gil had come to interview her.

'What's happened?' I said.

'That police inspector was here.'

'Oh no! He's been here already. There's a rumour in the village that those cadets found something in your cottage and I came to warn you that Rankin would probably come and I wanted you to give me a ring so I could come straight away to support you.'

'Thank you, Frank, but it wasn't anything he said to me that's upset me. I broke down after he'd left when I saw what had happened to Barnaby.'

'What's he done to Barnaby?' I said my anger rising. Where is he?'

'He's in his room and he won't come out. It's a serious setback for him.'

'The police have no mandate to destroy the delicate equilibrium of fragile people. Rankin's got to be made to face up to what he's done. He's a public servant, not a public inquisition.'

'It's not all his fault, it's partly mine. I brought Barnaby here for selfish reasons.'

'Selfish!' You couldn't have been more altruistic. You were doing a wonderful job building up his self-esteem. Look, Jean, I'm going to put on your jug and make a pot of tea and you can tell me what Chief Inspector Rankin did to upset Barnaby. We'll go over their confrontation together and we'll talk about getting Barnaby back on track.'

I poured her a cup of tea and was rewarded with a gentle smile that attempted to dry the tears that still dampened her eyes. At my prompting she recounted some of the details of Rankin's visit.

'First of all,' she said, 'he barged in and said he had a license to search the house.'

'He said license, not warrant?'

'No, license.'

'That means he didn't have a warrant. Go on.'

'He paid particular attention to Barnaby's room upsetting the manic order that Barnaby had established there. He found his camera in a drawer and he commented on its quality and wrote the details in his notebook. He checked to see what photos were in the camera and there weren't any. He said to Barnaby that if it was his camera there would be photos in it and he wanted to know why there weren't any photos. Barnaby just looked at him blankly.

'Next, he demanded to know where Barnaby's knapsack was, the one he'd been seen carrying when he went out walking. Barnaby hangs it on the back patio so I took the inspector out there. To Barnaby's increasing consternation he tipped everything out of it. There were the items you'd expect to find in the knapsack of a walker, a water bottle, insect spray, a compass, a packet of band aids and so on, but the bulkiest item and one that the inspector didn't expect to find was the coil of rope and tackle that Barnaby always carried with him,'

'What's all this?' he said.

'Barnaby wouldn't say anything so I explained that he used to be very interested in nature and he still is, but he doesn't climb trees or rock faces any more to inspect birds' nests and animal retreats, but he still carries the rope and tackle around because it's a sort of security blanket for him and one day he might use it again.

'The Inspector got really angry then and told me that Barnaby would never make any progress while I kept speaking for him. He said that there was one piece of information that he needed that only Barnaby knew and he was going to go walking with him so he could show him exactly where he picked up the pen. I told him that Barnaby wouldn't go with him unless I was there too and he said that I could come, but he'd be watching me to make sure that I didn't select a spot for him.

'We crossed the bridge and walked towards the forest and then we kept going right round to the other side. The inspector kept telling him that he didn't have to say anything at all and all he wanted him to do was to point to the spot where he picked up the pen. Barnaby stopped when he came to the caravan park fence, but he didn't point to any spot, he just stood there. I could see that he was deeply troubled and the inspector could see that it was the forest itself that was troubling him.'

'You went into the rain forest,' he said. ' The sign says keep out, but you went in. Look, Barnaby, that doesn't matter. Those signs should have been taken away years ago. We'll all go into the forest now and you can show me where you found the pen.'

'That was too much for Barnaby. He turned and bolted and I ran after him. The inspector didn't follow us. He just stood there looking at the tangle of vegetation.

'The inspector has a lot to answer for,' I said. 'He's barged in and seriously disturbed the psyche of a young man who's been struggling to find normality. No case is worth solving at such a price. You are left to pick up the pieces, Jean. I wish I could be more help to you.

'You do help me, Frank. Knowing that I'm not alone against the slings and arrows means a lot to-me. Barnaby's had a severe panic attack, but the psychiatrist has given me plenty of advice about dealing with those.'

'It takes a load off my mind knowing that the damage has not been irreversible. It mustn't happen again though. If the inspector turns up again, give me a ring and I'll be right over.'

'Thank you, Frank, I'll certainly do that.'

I left her then, tending to Barnaby while I went off to further my efforts to find the real criminals involved in the heist at No 122.

Chapter 10

B eing under cover in an investigation has its advantages, but the handicap that your clandestine status places on you is very frustrating. I was eager to follow up on any ex-prisoners who'd been accommodated at Green Acres, but the Correctional Services Department wouldn't be handing out information to any low-grade public servant. I was entirely dependent on Gil to get hold of prison records and parole reports and Gil seemed to be avoiding me.

Perhaps I'm misjudging him because I'm a little irate over his treatment of Barnaby. I know that he's a top detective and he wouldn't have not noticed the proximity of the caravan park to the forest that seemed to alarm Barnaby and by now he's probably organizing a thorough search of the whole area. He may well have the prison reports that I require, but he's holding off on them because of the protocol that ex-prisoners shouldn't be harassed. It's a pity that his sensitivity didn't extend to the mentally ill.

He's entitled to his opinion that my interest in Jean makes me a less than ideal person to investigate her, but the point is that I'm not investigating her at all. I'm concentrating my enquiry on Green Acres Caravan Park and I need to know who the ex-prisoners are so I can get to know them as I help Harold Hardaker with his coffee van. I expect that I won't be as good at serving coffee as Cody and Hank were, but they've moved on and I'm the only one who's likely to offer to replace them.

It's not surprising then that I made a priority of contacting Gil and I made my way to Rachael Parker's office rather than trust the aging Serendipity copper wires which could at the drop of a hat turn a private call into a party line affair. Gil was out of course when I rang, but I left my message with every confidence that he'd receive it.

While waiting for Gil to get back to me, I took the opportunity to question Rachael about the conference she promised to have with her staff concerning the master key.

'Have you and your staff come up with any situation where the master key could have been picked up for a minute and pressed into a block of wax before being put down again?' I said.

'We've been through this year's register,' she replied, 'and each of us could recall the times when we took the key out. No one, though, could come up with any compromising situations. On every occasion doors were opened and residents were let in without the key leaving the hands of any staff involved.'

'Are you quite sure that no staff member was deliberately omitting to mention any compromising incident to avoid the embarrassment of having been a catalyst in the robbery?'

'Yes, I'm quite sure. As a matter of fact I used that very word catalyst. I pointed out that the robbery could have been assisted by something that one of us unwittingly did, but we were by no means part of it. If we now have an opportunity to assist the police, we'll pick up a lot of credit for it. I'm quite sure that no one tried to hide anything.'

'I'm most grateful for the effort the staff have put in and I'll get Gil to pass on the thanks of the police department. Most of the investigating we do involves a lot of trudging up a lot of dry gullies, but it's all necessary.'

'There's one unlikely event I should tell you about if you don't mind dry gullies,' Rachel said. 'As I was closing the register, Chloe, our nurse, reminded me of an incident that happened last year. Chloe had asked me what the policy was for the treatment of people outside the village who just happened to be inside the village when they had an accident. My immediate response had been that if it wasn't something quite minor an ambulance should be called. When she told me what had happened, however, I agreed that she was right to have dealt with it herself.'

'Was It someone related to a resident? I think we'd expect that the nurse would be available to help a visiting family member in trouble,' I said.

'No it was a member of the clergy, or at least a missionary from one of the churches. It's our policy here to welcome all representatives of the clergy because they are involved in the lives of some of our residents and we treat them as ex-officio staff members.'

'You said missionary. You are not talking about one of the Mormons who were staying at the caravan park until recently?'

Yes, they were helping Harold Hardaker with the coffee van, and they'd come back here to help him wash it down and scrub up the food preparation area as is required by health regulations.'

'As a matter of fact, I've just been talking to Harold and he was saying how obliging they'd been and what a hit they were at the caravan park. He called them Cody and Hank,'

'Yes, they are real live saints. The Catholic Church doesn't have a monopoly on them. The Mormon Church is full of saints apparently. Its official name is the Church of Jesus Christ of Latter-Day Saints and not the Mormon Church.'

It's highly unlikely that they'd be organizing house break-ins, is it? How did our nurse get involved with them?'

'Oh, I didn't finish my story. When Harold arrived with the missionaries, he discovered that he didn't have his house Key and he rang the office. Chloe happened to be there and I sent her down with the master key. While she was opening the door one of the missionaries tripped over the hose and he injured his ankle. Chloe ran back to her golf buggy to get her first aid kit and she bound up the ankle to stop it swelling. It was very painful apparently and she went back to her office to get a crutch for him.'

'That was very thoughtful of her, but the important detail for our investigation concerns the master key. Did Chloe remember what she did with the master key while she was tending to the injury?'

Yes, she did. I'm afraid she just threw it on the seat of the buggy when she picked up the first aid case.'

'And what were Harold and the other missionary doing while she was attending to the injury?'

'Chloe was concentrating on what she was doing and couldn't really say. She supposed they were watching her wind the bandage on.'

'That's exactly the situation we are looking for where a clear opportunity is given for someone to pick up the key and get a wax impression. I'm glad you brought it up even if the people involved in that situation are all wrong. Harold Hardaker and church missionaries wouldn't be looking for opportunities to steal a master key and ransack a house.'

'That's what Chloe and I thought, so I'm sorry we haven't been able to give you any leads at all from our handling of the master key.'

'No, no, the key incident with Hardaker and the missionaries is a lead particularly when the missionaries would have had opportunities to relieve Hardaker of his house Keys so the master key would be needed. Even though the characters don't fit the scenario I'll keep an eye on Harold and I'll get character references from the Mormon church for Cody and Hank, and they should be able to tell me where they are now.'

I realized when I was saying it that I had a predilection for following up the most unlikely of leads except when it was Jean Reid and her nephew who were being investigated. My conviction that Jean and Barnaby were innocent was solid and I would no more contemplate investigating them than I would think of investigating myself.

After tea I drove over to Rode Road to the Latter-Day Saint Church that my Gregory's Street directory showed to be the closest to Green Acres. It was Youth night apparently because a number of teenagers were heading into the building. I asked one of them if the minister or priest was inside. He looked at me blankly for a moment before he realized who I was looking for.

'Oh you want to see the bishop,' he said.

'No, no,' I said. 'I just want to see the person who runs this church.'

'He's called the bishop. I'll take you to him.'

I was introduced to a man who looked nothing like a bishop. He was dressed in jeans and T-shirt, but if he could tell me about Cody and Hank, I was quite prepared to accept his dress. As it turned out he couldn't tell me about Cody and Hank because he didn't know them. They didn't worship at his church. I was immediately alerted to the possibility of a couple of ring-ins.

'It looks as though Cody and Hank aren't Latter-Day Saints at all. They're just using the Mormon cover to hide what they're really doing.'

'Not necessarily,' the bishop said. 'They could be travelling to a new mission or they could have completed their mission in Australia and they are taking a holiday before they return home.'

'Is there any way I could find out about them?' I said.

'You could try the Stake. They'll have all the records of the missionaries in Australia at the Stake.'

'The Stake?'

'Yes, it's our administrative unit. It's responsible for the six churches in this area. Our Stake office is in Bracken Ridge. There'll be someone there tonight if you want to follow-up your enquiry straight away.'

'Thank you. I noticed the Bracken Ridge church in the Street directory when I was looking for the one closest to Green Acres. Now I expect the man in charge there will be an archbishop.'

'We don't have archbishops. He's the Stake President.'

I'd been surprised by the use of such an unecclesiastical word like stake to describe an administrative unit of a church but when he coupled it with the completely secular position of president, I wondered if he might be playing games with me. All outcomes are possible in the mind of detective on the trail of truth.

'Forgive me for seeming to question what you say, but it seems to me an unusual title to give to an office of your church.'

'Why unusual?'

There's no ecclesiastic aura about it, no connection with church history, unless the original stake president presided over the burning at the stake of unbelievers.'

The bishop laughed. 'I can assure you we have never gone down that road. The reference is to the stakes that strengthened the ancient Hebrew church which needed staking because it was a tent.'

'Thank you, you've been most helpful. I've learnt a bit about your church even if I don't catch up with two of your missionaries.'

I found the Stake President to be just as helpful to me and my investigation as the Bishop had been. Not only did he have no record of missionaries called Cody and Hank staying at Green Acres, but when I described what they'd been doing there, he was confident that they were not Latter-Day Saints.'

'Fulfilling a mission is a rite of passage for a young Latter-day Saint,' he said. They are committed to a strict life style which includes everything from regular attendance at church and regular scripture study to adherence to a code of health and nutrition in which tea and coffee are prohibited. Not only did your Cody and Hank neglect to attend any church in the stake jurisdiction, but their involvement in serving tea and coffee to the community indicates that they were not familiar with the Latter-Day Saint lifestyle they were apparently attempting to emulate.'

I thanked the Stake President most sincerely for his observations and drove away from his Bracken Ridge church with all the elation that a break through gives a detective. My elation on this occasion , however, was boosted by the certainty that I could disperse the cloud of police suspicion that surrounded Barnaby and Jean Reid.

Tomorrow I would start my day at sunup and concentrate my search around the Caravan that had been used by the ersatz Mormons and hopefully with Barnaby's cooperation find the spot in the forest where he'd found the pen. I was certain that that spot would also lead to the hiding place for the stolen goods while they awaited their removal to clandestine markets far away from 122 Rosella Lane in Serendipity Gardens.

Chapter 11

I t was 10pm by the time I got back to Serendipity Gardens and I was surprised to find Gil's car parked in front of my cottage. Gil emerged from it as I pulled in to my driveway.

'I'm sorry about the late hour,' he said, 'but I need to bring you up to date with the Rosella Lane investigation and add anything you've come up with to the mix. I'll be leaving everything with inspector Matthews while I'm in Sydney at a seminar.'

'How long will you be gone?'

'A week. It's a cyber-crime seminar. They're trying to make us as computer savvy as the cyber crims we investigate.'

'It's about time the force skilled up in that area. There's too much going on to leave it to a few boffins to sort out. Come in and I'll put the billy on.'

It was a satisfying conference we had over our cup of tea and the scones I produced from the freezer, satisfying because we'd both made progress in our investigations. Gil had wasted no time getting back to the patch of remnant forest where Barnaby had refused to go in with him to point out where he'd picked up the pen. He'd returned within the hour with two constables, all three of them dressed in overalls to conduct a thorough search of the area.

'It's a very degraded patch of rain forest,' Gil said. 'Some of the growth is remnant: a few cabbage tree palms are original and the black bean has survived in patches, and there's a lot of Lily-Pilli there too and some Cottonwood, but the Camphor Laurel trees look like they're going to take over along with all the cat's Claw creepers and Morning Glory that's strangling the canopy.'

'You sound like a forest ranger examining a patch for rehabilitation. I suppose what you're saying is that it was too dense to penetrate.'

'It is dense and there was no point in trying to hack our way into it. That's why we concentrated on finding a track that had already been cut. It was well camouflaged at the entrance, but once we were in, we had no trouble following it to a small clearing where the earth seemed to have subsided leaving a depression about four feet deep that had been lined with leaves from the cotton trees that were all around it. It was clear from the planks of sawn timber and the plastic sheeting lying round that the depression had been used as a storage place.'

'From what you say, it could have been used to hide the loot from a number of break-ins. They seem to have gone to a lot of trouble to cut a path through a dense rain forest and dig a sizable hole and cover it with planks and no doubt cover the lot with forest litter.'

'Yes, it was a well-planned operation, but I don't think they had to dig that hole. To me, it looked more like a subsidence than a dug hole.'

'It would be unusual for the land to subside in the middle of a rain forest, wouldn't it?'

'Depends what's been dug out underneath it. During the war there were underground petrol tanks in this area that serviced the huge army camp at Chermside, but I understood that they were where the caravan park now is. You don't put petrol tanks under a rain forest.'

'Perhaps part of the rain forest was cleared, but it's now moved back into the cleared area.'

'You could be right, but thankfully it's not our job to investigate rain forest creep. All we have to know is that stolen items were hidden in there and if the skaters pen was found in there, we'll know for certain that's where the paintings and the silver ware and the other artifacts from Rosella Lane were hidden while they awaited disposal by whoever was fencing the stuff.'

'I suppose you'll be dragging Barnaby Reid in there to get a confession out of him for the part you imagine he played.'

'Barnaby Reid is no longer a suspect,' Gil replied.

'Why?' I said, knowing deep down that the circumstantial evidence was stacked against him.

'Because a report on the Reids came through from Queenscliff this afternoon. The Reids were known to the police there, but for all the right reasons. Joe and Jean Reid were part of the boating fraternity who were able to report on the movement of boats suspected of bringing drugs into the country.'

'And Barnaby was part of that exercise?'

'No, he had another skill that the police down there found useful on occasion. That was before his breakdown of course.'

'Jean said he was a rock climber and he used to climb tall trees as well.'

'Yes, that's what she said, but the Queenscliff police knew him as a speleologist. He didn't climb up, he climbed down into caves, and he was helpful to them when they needed someone who'd do that,'

'There's nothing to stop him being a rock climber and a speleologist. Anyway neither Barnaby nor his skills are in contention as far as the robbery is concerned. I know who carried out that job and they fit in nicely with the hidey hole you've discovered and Barnaby's panic when you wanted him to go into the rain forest. They probably found him hanging round there and warned him off in no uncertain terms. After all, the signs were saying it was a prohibited area,'

'Forget about Barnaby. You said that you knew who broke into No 122. Are you going to keep withholding information from me?'

'I'm not withholding information. I've just come back from a couple of interviews that have put the culprits in our sights. I haven't had a chance to tell you about them yet,'

I gave Gil a full rundown on Cody and Hank who were staying at the caravan park until recently pretending to be Mormons, and how I was prompted to check up on them when Nurse Chloe at the village remembered an incident that in all probability, they had engineered to enable them to make an impression of the Serendipity master key and how their goose was cooked when my checking revealed that they weren't known at any of the Mormon churches in the North Brisbane Stake.

After satisfying him on a few questions which involved one about the North Brisbane Stake, Gil congratulated me with some enthusiasm on the breakthrough I'd managed.

'All we have to do now is track them down,' he said 'I don't suppose there are any photos we can circulate?'

'Photos might be hard to come by,' I said. 'They would have been camera shy given their undercover status.'

'You said they were popular at the caravan park. Someone might have one.'

'I'll make discreet enquiries. I'll go ahead with my original intention to help with the coffee van. I'll put it around that I want to write an article about the van and photos would be helpful.'

'Good. Talking of photos, Those you took of the tire tracks in Telstra lane might prove useful. Forensics has identified them as snow tyre tracks. It would be helpful if we were able to concentrate our search in the Alpine Region.'

'I wondered when I was going to get that forensics report. You haven't been withholding information from me have you Gil?'

'Certainly not, Frank. I only got the report yesterday. You should know how slow the forensics lab is with non-urgent enquiries.

'Yes, I'm used to the regional forensics team prioritising homicide investigations. I'm quite happy not to be dealing with a homicide right on my doorstep.'

'You wouldn't get a chance to be involved anyway. In the metropolitan area, the homicide team takes over and it doesn't brook any interference from the rest of the police force.'

'Fair enough. I believe in experts being in charge of flying the plane and I like to be left alone to do my own thing anyway. I'll get hold of photos of our two suspects and drop them in to Inspector Matthews for distribution to all police stations and I'll also be looking for impressions of snow tyre treads in the caravan park or anywhere around that rain forest. If I find any, we may be able to zoom in on our suspects skiing on Mount Buffalo.'

'Yes, you never know where an investigation will lead. We start off with the Reverend Robert Walker skating on Duddingston Loch and we end up with two missionaries skiing on Mount Buffalo.'

Chief Inspector Gilbert Rankin was in good form and we continued on extracting scenarios from the evidence I'd collected. My bracket clock struck midnight before I was able to retire to bed.

Chapter 12

Despite my going to bed late, I woke early the following morning keen to get started with my search for tyre tracks, but there was one thing I wanted to do before I left the village. I wanted to see Jean and tell her about Cody and Hank who were now the prime suspects for the robbery. She would be relieved to hear that the police would be no longer interested in Barnaby and he could get on with his recovery without having to worry about any more police accusations and demands.

I wasn't sure how I was going to tell her because who was I to be in possession of breaking news from the police. I'd have to say I'd heard a rumour. Nobody knows where rumours start. Perhaps the Stake President mentioned something to a parishioner who rang someone in the village with this prime piece of gossip.

Jean was enjoying tea and toast on her back patio, but when she saw me, she got in first with the news that I was keen to bring to her.

'Barnaby's off the hook. He's no longer a suspect,' she said

'How do you know?' I said, not surprised by the news, but genuinely surprised that she knew.

'That Detective Inspector dropped a note in my letterbox late yesterday afternoon. It really gave me a lift. Here read it for yourself.'

I took the note and read it.

> *Dear Mrs Reid, Just wanted to let you know that you are no longer regarded as a suspect in the Rosella Lane case and neither is Barnaby. I apologise to you and Barnaby for putting you through that police interrogation, but I don't apologise for checking up on you. The Queenscliff police were more than grateful for the help that both of you had given to them and they left me in no doubt that you would not have been involved in breaking into a house. I apologise once again for any stress I put Barnaby under and I hope most sincerely that his recovery will be swift.*
>
> *Yours sincerely Gilbert Rankin*

'Well I'll be tarred and feathered,' I said when I read it. 'A personal apology from a policeman. I wonder how sincere that really is.'

'They are human beings; you'll have to learn to accept them.'

'Don't get me wrong, I'm happy that Detective Inspector Rankin has taken Barnaby off his suspect list, but I'll only trust him until the next time he starts riding roughshod over people.'

Jean laughed. 'You're very generous with your trust.'

I wanted to change the subject. I didn't want to tell her about Cody and Hank now that she knew that Barnaby was no longer a suspect. Gil and I and the Stake President were the only ones who knew about their duplicity and I wouldn't be doing my undercover status any favour by talking about it. I'd noticed what I thought to be sawdust scattered over the patio pavers so I selected the sawdust as my new topic.

'I see you have been doing some woodwork,' I said. 'You are a jack of all trades.'

'I've enough on my plate without starting woodwork,' she replied. 'That's there for the ants. I don't know what it is, but it's treated with some sort of insecticide that they take back to the nest and it kills all the ants there.'

'And it really works?'

'Like a charm. I put this stuff down a couple of days ago and they've all gone. I'll just sweep it into the cracks between the pavers and my house will continue to be an ant free zone.'

'Where did you get it from? The little blighters are trying to take over at my place too.'

'I's not on the market. One of our boating friends was an industrial chemist and he made it up. We found it very useful on the farm. I'd forgotten that I brought a couple of boxes with me until Barnaby came out of his room and said that there were ants all over his bed.'

'Your friend will make a fortune if he markets it.'

'I think that one of the insecticide company is running trials. They'll have to tick every safety box before they'll be allowed to sell it. I can give you some though if you can use it without putting children and pets at risk.'

'None of those at my place. My son, Troy, and his wife, Sulee, went off to America chasing their careers. My granddaughter will start life on the other side of the world.'

There, I'd done it. I was starting to talk about my family so soon after determining that my new life in the village would leave my former life in the past. I was particularly surprised that I was talking to Jean about Troy. Jean had no children and I'd been careful not to stir any feelings of lost opportunities for her. Jean's response, however, was Jubilant.

'Wonderful! Wonderful! Frank. You have a whole family in America. Troy and Sulee, what beautiful names.'

But that's as far as our conversation about my family got. Someone was calling out for me down at my house. It was Millie Mockridge and she seemed distressed. I ran out into the garden and called out to her.

'I'm over here Millie. What's happened?'

'It's awful,' she called running down to me. ' Martha rang Janine, a woman has been found across the creek, she's been stabbed. They think she's from the village.'

They were both crying and my tears weren't far from coming. I'd spent much of my adult life examining cadavers and extracting information from silent corpses that had ended their lives shouting their horror to the heavens, but I'd always managed to be objective. Not now though. The murder of someone in the village was like the murder of someone in the family. It was that close to home. We were more than neighbours. No matter how different we were from each other our village family ties united us.

Jean took Millie in and poured her a cup of tea.

'I'll go and see if I can get more information' I said.

'They won't let you anywhere near where it happened,' Millie said, her composure partly restored by the first sip of tea. 'There are police everywhere and they've put up a tent.'

I knew I wouldn't get anywhere near the crime scene. Homicide would make sure that was off limits. Pathologists would be in the tent with the body and forensic police would be scouring the area all guarded by constables who'd be making sure that nothing was contaminated by anyone who wasn't in the homicide team.

'I'll see what I can do,' I said and left to make a phone call. Rachael wouldn't be at work yet so I risked being listened to by a third party and used my house phone. The pressure was on me now to reactivate my mobile phone which I'd happily abandoned to suit my assumed lifestyle that favoured all the inconveniences of the good old days.

Fortunately Inspector Matthews was an early starter and I found him at work.

'Do you know anything about this murder in the park beside Serendipity village?' I said.

'Yes, the body was found by a cleaner from the supermarket going home from night shift. Homicide have been there since 4.30 this morning. Detective Inspector Sweetman is in charge and he's already picked up a full report on the robbery at Rosella Lane in case the homicide is linked to it.'

'They've identified the body then?'

'Yes, she had ID on her. Her name won't be released until they find her husband. You might be able to help there. His name's Ray Gasper.'

'Jane Gasper's dead!'

'Oh, you know them. I'm sorry,' he said.

I didn't know I had nerves in my stomach, but they responded now to the news of Jane's murder and I knew that my vocal cords would be choked with emotion, but I forced a response.

'Jane Gasper was everyone's favourite person,' I said and I added incongruously, 'she could strum a Ukulele perfectly. The village will be devastated.' My voice broke on the 'devastated' and I hung up.

I wanted to be more composed when I returned to Jean and Millie so I headed for the office holping that news of the disaster had reached Rachael and she'd come to work early to deal with it.

I found her in her office with coffee and toast supplied by the restaurant. After a few moments of mutually consoling phrases, we got down to the business of finding Ray Gasper.

'The police got me out of bed this morning with the horrible news. They wanted to know if I knew where Ray Gasper was. I came straight in to check our register of people absent from the village.'

'And Ray recorded in the register that he wasn't going to be here last night?'

'Yes, he's been away two nights and he's not due back for another two.'

'That still doesn't tell us where he is now.'

'No, but that's not the purpose of the register. It's there to enable us to conduct an accurate roll call in the event of some disaster like a fire, but if he's recorded that he's going to be away, someone in the village probably knows where he is.'

'Did the Gaspers have a close circle of friends?'

'I've jotted down half a dozen people who might be able to tell us where he's gone. If you ring three and I ring three, it will be easier on us. They won't be easy calls or short calls and we might have to fall back on some counselling skills.'

We got the job done and I suppose we helped some of the people we called to cope with the news, but we didn't find out where Ray Gasper was staying. We only knew that he'd gone to Sydney on business. I didn't get to search for tyre tracks that day either. When I got back to Jean's place to break the news about Jane Gasper, the house was in turmoil. Barnaby had been taken away and the nurse was there to treat Jean for shock and Millie and Janine, who'd been called in by Millie, were both in a state of near collapse or at least Millie was. Janine retained some self-control and was trying to comfort her friend.

Following hard on my heels the doctor arrived. Nurse Chloe had called him to prescribe the sedative that would allay Jean's consuming distress and deliver the balm of sleep to her for the rest of the day.

Chapter 13

I kissed Jean on the forehead as she drifted off and then I sat Millie and Janine down at the dining room table to extract from them their version of what had happened. Janine immediately cut to the chase with her pejorative summary.

'Detective Inspector Sweetman arrested Barnaby Reid for the murder of Jane Gasper. Jean now has to face up to reality. Barnaby is no good. Nobody deserves a relative like Barnaby and the sooner he's locked up and Jean can forget about him the better.'

'Inspector Sweetman just came in and arrested him?' I said failing to bring to mind any rational basis for such an arrest.

'No, no,' Millie cut in, 'He showed everyone his police card and said he wanted to talk to Barnaby, but Jean said he was asleep and she wasn't going to wake him. He said that a woman had been murdered and he needed to question Barnaby,'

'You could see that that really upset Jean,' Janine said taking up the story. 'She asked him what gave him the right to come into her house and accuse Barnaby of being a murderer, and he said that Barnaby had already come to the notice of the police and he had a duty to check what he was doing last night.'

'Jean really believed that Barnaby couldn't possibly have murdered anyone and she didn't like the police insinuating that he had,' Millie said taking up the story again. 'She told him straight out that if he didn't have a warrant to be in her house, he was to get out immediately.'

'Fortunately the Inspector wasn't intimidated,' Janine said. 'He started looking around and when he saw Barnaby's knapsack hanging out on the patio, he took it down to see what was in it. When he pulled out the blood-stained knife, the house was plunged into chaos. Jean screamed, Barnaby came running from his bedroom, Inspector Sweetman called in the two constables who were waiting outside and Jean tried to get between Barnaby and the Inspector. One of the constables held her while Inspector Sweetman arrested her nephew for the murder of Jane Gasper.'

'That was the first time we heard who the murdered woman was,' Millie pointed out. 'It came as a terrible shock to us. I know I cried out and every muscle in my body was reduced to putty. I had to sit down.'

'It was a complete calamity for Jean,' Janine said. 'When Detective Inspector Sweetman said that it was Jane Gasper Barnaby had murdered she collapsed and the constable had to carry her into her bedroom. It was lucky for her that she did collapse. She didn't have to watch the other constable handcuffing Barnaby and marching him out to the police car. It was chilling, he didn't show any emotion at all. He was a cold-blooded murderer and he sent shivers down my spine.'

'We went into the bedroom then to see what we could do for Jean. The Inspector came in too and told me to call the nurse and I pushed the button on the vita-call. By the time the nurse came Jean was conscious and she was sobbing. The Inspector had a few words with the nurse and she called the doctor.'

They'd given me a blow-by-blow description of what had happened and even though Janine in particular saw Barnaby as the devil incarnate, I thanked them both for being there for Jean. I told them that they'd have my gratitude for life if they could take it in turns to stay by her bedside until she woke up. The nurse no doubt would be checking on her from time to time, but I didn't want her left alone at any time.

I said that I'd be back by the time she woke, but it was essential for me to go into the police headquarters to try to find out what was happening to Barnaby because that was the first thing Jean would want to know when she woke. I added that both Jean and I knew that Barnaby was completely innocent of the murder.

They promised to organize the bedside vigil, but I'm sure that Janine for one didn't share my conviction that Barnaby hadn't stabbed Jane Gasper.

I parked my car in the carpark at the Roma Street Police Headquarters and looked at the drab and forbidding building that housed the multitude of sections charged with catching criminals and presenting them to Judges and magistrates all decked out with the evidence that was needed to lock them up. If I hadn't resisted, I could have ended up in a place like this, a pressure cooker place where those charged were cooked quickly to make room for the job of fixing the next one for the pot. Don't get me wrong, though, I am not being critical of my colleagues. Given the pressure, they do an excellent job here. My resisting the transfer I was offered wasn't down to any aversion to a quick fix to speed up the delivery of justice. How could it have been when I myself destroyed evidence I'd collected to protect three people from murder convictions.

From what Inspector Matthews had said Detective Inspector Sweetman had that narrow focus on making quick arrests and he didn't take kindly to any criticisms of the judgements he'd made. I knew that to secure the best outcomes for Barnaby I'd have to avoid any direct confrontation with him.

After waiting fifteen minutes, I was shown in to Detective Inspector Sweetman's office to be greeted quite affably.

'Frank Coleman,' he said holding out his hand, 'the legend from Central Queensland, Your reputation precedes you.'

'Apparently. I was looking forward to a quiet retirement at Serendipity Gardens, not the stress of undercover policing there.'

'Nevertheless, Gil Rankin made a good move roping you in. I see that you are well on the way to catching the house breaker.'

'We know who was responsible but we're still a long way from finding them.'

'You may have your hands full then. There's no need for me to point out that you've been contracted to deal with the one issue at Serendipity Gardens and you won't be needed to investigate the murder.'

'Do you think that I'm itching to do that?'

'I hope you aren't. It's just that Inspector Matthews said that you and Gil Rankin had eliminated Barnaby Reid from the list of suspects in the robbery and you might be looking to do the same for the murder charge.'

'Have you charged him with murder?'

'Not yet. We've charged him with being a danger to the public. It'll be upgraded to murder as soon as forensics identifies his finger prints on the knife.'

'If there are finger prints on the knife,' I said.

'Hold on a minute, before I insult you by telling you that I can't discuss the investigation with you because you're not on the investigating team, I want to ask you one question. If you were investigating the stabbing of a woman and a mentally unstable man was there with a blood-stained knife in his possession, would you or would you not take the man into custody?'

'I'd have taken him into custody, of course. There would have been a public outcry if he'd been left in the community.'

'That's settled then. You're not going to demand that he be released.'

'Not at all. You've got him in a holding cell?'

'Yes, he'll stay there until he's charged with the murder and the guilty verdict is pronounced.'

'I know you don't want to hear me say this, but I can't help myself. What if there are no prints on the knife to tie him to the murder? You can't hold him and not charge him with a serious crime without some lawyer demanding his release. Wouldn't it be better to put him in a psychiatric ward now? That's where he'll most likely end up if he's found guilty.'

'Put him in ward 15! That would stir up the do-gooders. He's not a prisoner, they'll say and you've lumped him in with all the addicts, psychos, and suicidal maniacs who can't be looked after in jail.'

'I don't mean ward 15, I mean the general psychiatric ward.'

'They're going to welcome him there aren't they, a homicidal maniac mixing with people who are in for depression or seeing things that aren't there.'

'All psychiatric patients are capable of violence. Anything that could be used as a weapon is confiscated and the ward is kept locked which suits the needs of a prisoner on remand.'

'I'll give some thought to that if there are no prints on the knife and the lawyers want him released. It will be up to the courts to decide what accommodation he gets when his guilt is proven.'

'Is Barnaby Reid saying anything about his guilt or innocence?'

'Barnaby Reid is saying nothing. He hasn't uttered a word since he was taken into custody, not to us, not to the duty solicitor, and not to the Salvo who's trying to fulfil his duty of care.'

'I don't like the sound of that. There'll be a media witch hunt if there's a death in custody.'

'I'll put him on suicide watch, but the sooner he's out of my hair the better.'

'You can get a court order to transfer him to a psychiatric ward. That would put him right out of your hair.'

'Would it? It will more likely increase the work load. They'd be suspicious that we were trying to fix his trial by presenting him as a loony.'

'You'd have to put a case and they'd have their psychiatrist examine him, but I'd be willing to follow it through if you assigned me the task.'

Chief Inspector Sweetman laughed.

'I have a $50 wager with Inspector Matthews that you won't be successful in securing the release of Barnaby Reid. He's lost the wager. You're not interested in his release, only making sure that he survives to stand trial. You go after that court order by all means and have him ready for his appointment with the judge sound in wind and limb, if not mind.'

I thanked the Chief Inspector for authorizing me to negotiate with the court, but I didn't tell him that he would actually be losing his wager because he would be releasing Barnaby when I tracked down the real murderer.

I spent most of the day that was left securing Barnaby's release from the police cell and his transfer to the psychiatric ward at the General Hospital and I got back to Jean just before she woke.

Travelling back to Serendipity, I gave a lot of thought to helping her through the nightmare of her waking. I came to the conclusion that I would have to be completely honest with her. Barnaby's release from the police cell could only have been achieved from inside the police force and my continuing efforts to free him completely would only build confidence in her if she saw that my efforts had full police backing. My dream of establishing a new life that had no link to Inspector Coleman's cadavers would have to be compromised.

Chapter 14

'Barnaby's in hospital! What did those bastards do to him!' That was how Jean responded to my news that Barnaby had been taken from the police cell and admitted to the hospital ward. She had not fully emerged from the numbing fog that had engulfed her mind when the medication kicked in. She came now through the mists of her forgetting, struggling to make sense of what she was seeing. The shadows of the evening suggested to her the grey pre-dawn light and she wanted to know why I was there so early. It had been a hot night for her and finding herself lying on top of the bed and not in it, she was impelled by her modesty to see that her night dress was in place. She wasn't wearing a night dress, of course. She was still in the T-shirt and skirt she'd put on when she got up that morning. She looked at me with a puzzled, almost an accusing expression.

'It's not morning, Jean. It's the end of the day. You need to remember what happened this morning.'

She stumbled out of the fog then and hit a glass wall that knocked her down into the horror of Barnaby's arrest. She was off the bed and leaning against the wardrobe sobbing and her words rose fitfully to the surface.

'They... accused Barnaby... of murder. They said he murdered... Jane Gasper... Jane Gasper is... dead! How could they accuse Barnaby? He didn't even know her. Where did they take him? ... Did you find out where they took him Frank?'

'Yes, I went into the police headquarters in Roma Street to find out what was happening to him. They had him in a holding cell there, but his condition was a cause of concern. He'd withdrawn completely into his silent world so they've transferred him to the hospital where...'

'Barnaby's in hospital! What did those bastards do to him!' Jean cut me off before I was able to mention the Psychiatrists in the mental health ward.

'No, no.' I said, 'the police did nothing to him. He's been admitted to the Psychiatric ward where they've stabilized him. The hospital contacted his Psychiatrist in Queenscliff and they've got everything under control.

'Thank God,' she said regaining her composure. Did Inspector Rankin intervene? Did they drop the charges?

'No, Gil Rankin is still in Sydney, but the charge will be dropped. Look Jean, Nurse Chloe will be here shortly to check that you're OK and she'll be bringing the dinner that I've ordered from the restaurant. We can relax while we're eating and I'll take the opportunity to tell you something confidential that you need to know.'

'Knowing that the murder charge will be dropped puts anything else I need to know in the shade.'

'Trust me you need to know what I'm going to tell you.'

She took my hand and stroked it and her eyes were moist and her voice was soft with sincerity. 'I trust you, Frank. I've never had a better friend. Thanks for everything.' Then she smiled, 'Everything includes this dinner that's coming, You don't know how hungry I am.'

'Understandable, you haven't eaten all day.'

'And I need a shower and a change of clothes.'

'Good, you attend to your needs and I'll set the table.'

The nurse arrived with her medical bag and covered dishes from the restaurant. Jean was in the bedroom getting dressed and she went in and chattered to her and performed various little tests known to nurses before pronouncing her fit and well. She came out and put a couple of the restaurant dishes in the preheated oven. She seemed to be in no hurry to leave and she stayed talking to me as I pushed a Brown Brothers Late harvest Moscato into the ice bucket and stood a Coonawarra Estate Merlot beside it.

Jean emerged from the bedroom then and everything changed around her. A curtain had gone up and she entered the stage, a leading lady presented for audience approval. I hadn't seen that dress before, such charm radiating from such simplicity. I was spellbound, I could only murmur, 'You look so beautiful, Jean.'

The nurse laughed and clapped her hands. 'I know I'm intruding, but I had to stay and catch Frank's reaction to that dress. It's perfection on you , Jean, but I've become part of a crowd, I'd better go back to being a nurse. Enjoy your dinner.'

Jean thanked her for being such a friend and we were left alone to enjoy the company we were both beginning to cherish.

We were well into the sweet and sour pork dish before I got around to telling her about my former life and my current role at Serendipity. She was quiet when I finished and I looked at her keen for her response. Finally she gave it.

'I can't tell you how thankful I am that you are a police inspector and you've been there for Barnaby. You got him the care he couldn't do without and you'll be continuing to investigate the murder until the right person is behind bars.'

I couldn't help noticing the hesitation and hearing sentences crafted for an official she'd just met. Where was the Jean who just a while ago had held my hand and called me the best friend she'd ever had? I was silent for a while before I responded.

'Thank you, Jean, I appreciate what you just said, but you said it so formally. I've been sitting here just wanting to give you a big hug. A while ago you took my hand and let me know what you felt. There was no feeling for me in your little speech to a police officer.'

'I'm sorry, Frank, but you are suddenly a different person from the one I was developing an affection for. You were satirical and you looked at life through a philosophical lens and you were never pejorative. You were an advocate for keeping the police in their proper place to give everyone the freedom to enjoy the lifestyle that appealed to them, and I really believed that you liked playing the Ukulele. How much of that was just a front to support your undercover role?'

'Nothing was a front, Jean. The way you found me is the real me. I want you to know that. When I came to Serendipity and realized that I could discard all the chafing accoutrements of the police force I felt free for the first time in my adult life. I wasn't easily talked into the undercover role and I only accepted when I realized how important it would be for me to play the role of the real me and not that of a policeman. In this village you and Rachael are the only ones who know that I was ever a policeman and I hope you'll be able to forget that even when you are reading the book I'm thinking of writing. It won't be easy because the main character in the book will be a policeman.'

'You're going to write a book about your life in the police force! How do you expect not to be recognized in the Village?'

'I'll be writing it as a work of fiction and I'll be adopting a pseudonym.'

'That is the craziest thing I've heard since I came to Serendipity.'

'Why crazy? You don't think me capable of writing a book? Is it my over-reaching expectation that you can't accept?'

'Of course not, Frank. What's so fluky that it's crazy is that you are planning a book and I have one with a publisher. It will be out in time for the Christmas market this year, yet neither of us knew that the other was a writer.'

'I haven't revealed that I'm a writer because I haven't written anything yet and when I do write, I'll be somebody else, but how is it that you've never spoken about a book of yours that's about to come on the market?'

'Because I've strict instructions from the publisher not to say anything about it. I wanted to tell you about it so you'd understand my guilt about Barnaby and why he was so evasive about where he'd found the pen. I asked the publisher if I could tell you in strict confidence and he said, tell nobody. He'll tell me now how right he was when he finds out that you're a policeman,'

'What on earth did you write about that requires such secrecy?'

'The book contains material that will stir up a good deal of public interest and the publisher doesn't want investigative journalists stealing all its thunder before it hits the market.

'You've really hit the jackpot with your writing. You've selected a topic that the public won't be able to resist apparently, but what intrigues me is that it impacts on the pen that Barnaby found.

'Yes, it does and now that I know that you are the police officer who's championed Barnaby's innocence, I'm confident that I can trust you with my story no matter what the publisher says. I need you to understand what was going on with Barnaby more than I need to keep faith with my publisher.

You can be quite confident, Jean, that your publisher's need for secrecy will not be compromised by anything you tell me. The police don't broadcast confidences. Any light you shine on Barnaby's activity won't be made public, but it will help to allay any suspicion that Inspector Sweetman might have that Barnaby's a thief and a murderer.'

We finished our creamed rice and peaches dessert and Jean suggested that we move over to the lounge chairs. She said that if we were to get to know each other I would need to hear her story and Barnaby's involvement in it. She added that it was a longish story and we might as well be comfortable. I asked her if she wanted her wine glass refilled, but she said that she was ready to talk and she didn't need any more wine to loosen her tongue. I was about to learn a lot more about Jean and that had me so focused that I left my empty wine glass on the table.

Chapter 15

W ithout any further ado, Jean started her story as soon as she sat
down.

'I joined the Australian Women's Army Service (the AWAS) in 1941 and
was placed in the signals unit, but I was soon involved with Radar Surveillance
and was transferred to Townsville where a group of AWAS were keeping a
watch for Japanese planes. Radar was a new technology and we were sworn to
secrecy about our operation.

'I didn't stay in that job very long though. I was sent back to the AWAS
camp here at Chermside, but to my surprise and increasing dismay I wasn't
accommodated with the Signals Unit. I found myself in the transport
barracks with the women who were learning to drive the big army trucks.
They practiced all over Marchant Park that was kept free for that purpose.
I was disappointed because I'd begun to imagine that I had skills that were
more technological than mechanical. My pride took another blow the day
after I arrived when a driver turned up to take me to my new posting, We
came to the petrol dump about five miles north of the army camp and what
I saw depressed me further. The place looked deserted and the petrol drums
scattered around looked as though they'd been left behind during the chaos of
a hasty retreat. The petrol tanker dosing under the Camphor Laurel tree gave

the impression that it had been left there deliberately after it had discharged its last load into the underground tanks. At this stage I'd had no orders and the thought that I was being moved from the vital radar watch in Townsville to watch over the refurbishment of a derelict petrol dump a thousand miles from the front line fuelled my depression with gross servings of ennui. The donger, that looked as though it was being rejected by the jungle of trees behind it didn't help my mood, I'd be spending the rest of the war keeping records in there. I'd be recording petrol in and petrol out and breaking the monotony every now and then by using some unwieldly dip stick to measure levels in tanks.

My driver handed me over to a sergeant who appeared at the door of the donger. I felt like a parcel being delivered rather than an officer, no matter how low ranking, being welcomed to a new posting. The sergeant led me past a dusty and deserted counter down a dustier and bearer corridor. I was about to voice my dismay over the blatant neglect of military efficiency when the sergeant's demeanour changed. He stopped In front of a small door, sprang to attention and offered me a brisk salute.

'I stepped through the door, not into an office as I expected, but into a small cubicle. He followed me in, the door closed and we started to descend. I was confused and I struggled to rationalize the necessity for an elevator in a donger. I asked the sergeant if we were going down to the petrol tanks. 'There are no petrol tanks, Mam,' he replied. I soon discovered how right he was. We stepped out into a busy workplace full of uniformed men and women and the equipment that occupied them, typewriters, and the telex machines with their keyboards as well as the still familiar T38 morse keys. Nothing was being left to chance to send and receive the messages that fed the maps and charts scattered around the room.

'I was to become part of all this activity, but then I didn't comprehend how vital everything was to the defence of Australia. The sergeant led me straight through all of it down a hallway to a door that advertised that the person inside was Major General William Martin. His name on the door only increased my confusion about what was going on. What was a two-star general doing hiding behind a run-down petrol-dump, that wasn't a petrol-dump at all, to supervise everything? My briefing with the General established that a top-secret mission was afoot and I was to be part of it.

'From now on I'll just give you the facts. That huge bunker was to be the headquarters for the first confrontation with the Japanese army on Australian soil should they continue their so far unstoppable push southward through the islands. They would be stopped at Brisbane. The army called the big Brisbane defence build-up the Brisbane line.'

'Hold on, Jean, the Brisbane line was a myth spread around after the war to hurt the Labour party. A Royal Commission was called and it concluded that never at any stage did the Government ever consider handing over the northern part of Australia or any part of Australia to the Japanese.'

'The Royal Commission got it right. The Brisbane line was never a government decision. It was established by Field Marshall Blamey and General MacArthur as a military tactic. The Prime Minister and The Leader of the Opposition were advised, but it wasn't discussed in Parliament. North Queensland wasn't to be defended except to ensure that the population had a chance to move south. The Japanese push southward, however, would be suddenly halted at the Brisbane Line. The Army and the Air Force would have all the resources to make victory a certainty and it would be achieved without the months even years of bloodshed and destruction of infrastructure that would be the legacy of fighting the Japanese every inch of the way through the length of Queensland.'

'Thank God the Brisbane line you say was a reality was never needed. The Japanese were halted in the Coral Sea.'

'We didn't relax because we won the Coral Sea battle. We took on the responsibility of war propaganda. All reports from the front were vetted in our bunker.'

'Your book is becoming more interesting by the minute.'

'I hope you find it interesting, but the book isn't really what you want to find out about tonight, You want me to shine a light on what Barnaby was doing.'

'Yes Please. He needs all the help he can get. He's been suspected of theft and he's been taken into custody following a murder.'

'As far as the theft is concerned, I can tell you in confidence exactly where he found that pen. It was down in the bunker.'

'Down in your Brisbane Line defence bunker?'

'Yes. Barnaby thought it must have been left over from the war. There have always been biros around in his life time, but they hadn't been invented in the 1940s. I've no idea how it got down there.'

'I know how it got down there, but how did Barnaby get down into the bunker?'

'It's more appropriate to ask why he was down in the Bunker.'

'I'll ask why and how then.'

'Before his illness Barnaby was an expert speleologist. He'd been stable for about six months and I asked him if he thought he could go down into an underground cavern and take photos, flash photos for my book. I needed proof that there were white-washed plaster walls in the bunker to demonstrate clearly that it wasn't an excavation for a petrol dump. Barnaby accepted the challenge and I stressed the need for secrecy. That was a big mistake on my part because the secrecy became an obsession with him. He believed that everyone was out to extract the secret from him. He was naturally reserved, but now he was clamming up all together when strangers were around as he did when Inspector Rankin tried to get him to enter the rainforest to show him where he picked up the pen. That was getting far too close to the secret chamber and he bolted, not because of any guilt about a secret chamber, but because of his delusion that he had vital information to protect.'

'Poor Barnaby. I think he's now seeing his incarceration as another police ploy to extract information from him and he's fighting them with absolute silence.'

'I hope and pray that the psychiatrist will be able to undo the damage I've done.'

'You'll have to stop blaming yourself for Barnaby's condition. Your publisher triggered it when he demanded that you say nothing about the bunker before your book was published and the police poured oil on the fire by taking him into custody.'

'I can hardly blame the publisher; he's putting a lot of money into my book and he has a right to a market that hasn't been muddied by the articles of investigative journalists. I have to accept that I overestimated Barnaby's capacity to do the job I asked him to do.'

'No you didn't. He did the job you asked him to do didn't he?'

'Yes, he did; he got down into the bunker and the photos he took were perfect.'

'Getting down into the bunker must have been a feat in itself; there doesn't appear to be any obvious way in.'

'No, the place was evacuated and the entrances sealed after the war, but I remembered the ventilation shaft that surfaced in the forest. We took a couple of days to locate it because there was nothing left above ground anymore and the entrance to the shaft was a tangle of morning glory vine. It was narrower than I remembered, but Barnaby managed to push his way through it and drop down into the chamber with his ropes. I don't know how people can get any joy out of speleology.'

'Barnaby didn't have any inhibition about descending to the underworld?'

'No, the task activated him, and his description and photos of what he saw excited me because they matched so well my memory of the way things were.'

'I don't suppose he told you exactly where he found the pen down there.'

'No, but he gave me a rough idea. It was up towards the caravan park end of the chamber closer to the wall on the left. He said he was looking in the direction of the Caravan Park and the pen was lying on some rubble on the floor.'

'That's amazing. He's located it perfectly.' I told her about the depression in the forest floor that Gill Rankin suspected was a hiding place for stolen goods. I was certain now that it was, and the Skaters pen that had fallen from it down into the chamber below was proof positive that the stolen goods had come from 122 Rosella Lane.'

Now that Jean knew that I was a policeman, there was no point in keeping anything from her. I told her about Cody and Hank and how we would go about tracking them down. I also assured her that I'd be going after Jane Gasper's real murderer who'd be thrown into prison with no hope of ever getting out. I knew that my assurances were over confident because Detective Inspector Sweetman wouldn't be making any forensic evidence available to me or any other police resources for that matter, but I justified my boasting with the thought that at 11pm on the day that Barnaby was arrested, Jean was confident that I'd be able to put the matter right.

Chapter 16

Was it only yesterday morning that I was thinking that Jane Gasper's murder would see the village united? One of our family had been struck down and the shock waves would bind us all in a determined purpose to see the malicious assailant jailed for life. I couldn't have been more wrong. Twenty-four hours later the village was split and raw acrimony flowed in the lanes.

Roger Masters arrived at Jean's front door to protect her from what he called the conventional folly of do-gooders in the community. A group of Serendipity residents had descended on the village office and demanded that Rachael expel Jean Reid from the community. She had harboured a house breaker who had gone on to murder and her own involvement in the crimes must surface as the police pursued their investigations.

Roger said that the petitioners for Jean's expulsion had the blind mentality of a lynch mob, but unlike them, he didn't reach his conclusions without the application of logic to his observations.

'They're crazy,' I said. 'They've always tossed accusations around that are based on no evidence at all. They accused Jean of theft because they thought Queenscliff was just over the border and if she's guilty of theft she must be guilty of murder. They don't need evidence.'

'No, prejudice is enough for them,' Roger said, 'and prejudice is fed by emotional upsets. It's important that we understand where they're coming from. Ray Gasper phoned his wife from Sydney and not getting any answer he phoned one of her friends to be plunged into the Slough of Despond by the devasting news she had to pass on to him. It would have been a terrible phone call for both of them and the emotional devastation of it would have spread quickly to their group. It's not difficult to picture them shouting at Rachael that Ray Gasper would be back tonight and they wanted the Reid woman out of the village to spare Ray the trauma of the devil ridden reek of her presence.'

I looked at Jean, shocked that Roger should be repeating such vilification in her presence. ' You're not helping Jean, Roger, by repeating what those low life scuttle butts are saying.'

'I need to say it as it is , Frank, to convince her that the mood outside is dangerous. It's a minority mood now, but they'll be fanning the flames. Jean should not leave her cottage and if there is an absolute need to go out one of us should be with her.'

Jean accepted being talked about while she was there and she thanked Roger for letting her know what was going on and she assured him that she had work to do that was more important to her than embroiling herself in the rantings of vigilantes.

I thanked Roger for his forthrightness and for offering his services as a bodyguard.

'I take it that Rachael isn't contemplating evicting Jean,' I said.

'No, from what I hear she made it quite clear that Jean Reid had not been accused of any crime and even if she had been, she would be deemed innocent until proven guilty and it wasn't Serendipity policy to evict innocent people. She was supposed to have added That if Jean Reid was annoying her neighbours with excessive noise and bad language, or if she was spreading slander about other residents, she would certainly look into it. It was a well delivered rebuff, but one that could stir them to take matters into their own hands.'

'They'll have me to contend with if they come knocking on this door,' I said

Immediately there was a determined knocking on the front door galvanizing each of us as we braced for the confrontation with the rabble outside. I took a deep breath and opened it. I relaxed completely when I found only one person there. It was Millie Mockridge with a worried look that also melted away when she saw the three of us inside.

'You've heard about what's happening in the village,' she said with some urgency.

'Yes, I said. 'I thought the trouble had arrived when you knocked.'

'I've had a falling out with Jennine Rumble. She didn't want to get involved, but I want you to stay, Jean, and I want you to know that.'

'Thank you, Millie,' Jean said. 'Join us for a cup of tea and we'll talk about what's happening. Frank unfortunately can't stay. He has to go and find out about Barnaby.'

I took Jean's dismissal as an opportunity to slip away, but I went with the worrying thought that I was leaving Jean when she most needed me, a worry that was quite unnecessary as it turned out. Rachael had phoned Gil Rankin who sent a constable out to guard Jean's house. He stepped out into the middle of the road as the righteous enforcers of the law came into the laneway. The attempt to slander Jean out of house and home was deferred.

Chapter 17

As keen as I was to find a way into my investigation of Jane Gasper's murder, I was still committed to finding Cody and Hank and bringing them to justice for the Rosella Lane robbery. I went straight to the Caravan Park where Harold Hardaker was nearing the end of his morning coffee service. I didn't help him because I was too busy talking to his customers, particularly the women. What struck me was that here at the caravan park two criminals were held in the highest regard while in the retirement village two decent people who pulled their weight as citizens were judged to be criminals.

It was fortunate that Cody and Hank were held in high regard because one of the women actually had photos that she'd taken of them despite their request that none be taken because as missionaries they shrank from any sin of vanity that might be ascribed to them. The photos weren't taken full on, but their side view as they chatted to people would do very well for identification purposes. I promised to return the photos as soon as I had them copied.

Respect for Cody and Hank extended to the Caravan Park manager who approved of my project and handed me the key of the van they had occupied. It had just been returned by a departing overnighter and the van hadn't yet been cleaned. I declined his offer to send someone down to tidy up before I took my photos claiming that the lived-in look was just what I needed.

The van was easily located. It was the one on the southern end of the line of vans along the rainforest fence. I didn't bother opening it. There would be nothing of Cody and Hank left inside after weeks of changing occupancy with all the cleaning involved. I came to look for tyre tracks, not the tracks of their bicycle tyres, but the distinctive snow tyre tracks left by the vehicle of a visitor they might have had. I took a while to locate them because there was no sign of them beside the van. I had to follow the fence down to the corner where it changed direction to follow the creek. There they were, under the branches of a giant Camphor Laurel tree that reached over the fence from the rain forest. I had to use the flash on my camera to get photos of them.

Why was I so excited to find them? They were as close to the vans along the creek bank as they were to the vans along the rain forest fence and they didn't give any indication of the sort of vehicle they belonged to and if it was just a visiting vehicle there would be no registration number recorded in the Park office.

I was excited because that crazy pattern of ribs and channels that wandered all over the tyre tread like a dog's breakfast left their mark in Telstra lane around the corner from a Serendipity exit doorway. To find them again in the soft soil under a Camphor Laurel tree just down the fence from Cody and Hank's van gave a link to the Rosella Lane robbery and an assurance that I was on the right track with my investigation.

I was happier still after my conversation with the owner of the service station between Serendipity and the Caravan Park. I went in to pay for my petrol and the thought came to me to ask about snow tyres.

'I saw some strange tyre tracks over at the Caravan Park today, Julius, ribs and deep valleys wandering all over the place.'

'They sound like snow tyres, Frank.'

'Snow tyres! They're a bit out of their territory up here, aren't they?'

'We get 'em occasionally. Caravans don't have any boundaries. We serviced a vehicle with snow tyres three or four weeks ago. Joel the apprentice did the service and he'd never seen snow tyres before. He called me over to have a look at them.'

'What sort of vehicle was it?'

'To tell the truth I didn't take much notice of the vehicle. Joel will know, I'll call him.'

Joel left the vehicle he was working on and came into the shop. He had no hesitation in naming the vehicle with the snow tyres. It was a 1990 Toyota dual cab Ute.

'You know your cars,' I said to the apprentice.

'I'm getting to know them,' he said.

I thought of asking Julius if his office girl was as efficient as his apprentice and if she could check her records to find the registration number of the dual cab Ute with the snow tyres, but that would be putting my undercover role at risk. I'd let Inspector Matthews do the searching. A policeman doing police business wouldn't need any excuses to track down a criminal through the registration number of his vehicle and I would be free to concentrate my effort on bringing Jane Gasper's murderer to justice.

Chapter 18

Since Jane Gasper's murder, I've been drifting off to sleep at night with a mind full of spurious images of a crime scene I was not permitted to visit. I was denied any opportunity to look at the record carried by the surrounding ground or examine the aspects of the body and its fatal knife wound or to view the blood-stained knife itself. Now that I was ready to commence my investigation in earnest, I had no firm starting point, just the few general observations that had made their way to my notebook.

> * *A murder in a public park could be a chance killing by a deranged soul or it could a planned execution by a killer with a goading motivation.*
> * *In either case can't see the murderer as one of the residents of Serendipity village.*
> * *However, with the murder weapon targeting Barnaby by turning up in his knapsack, the murderer must surely be someone who is familiar with the village and recent events here.*

I read what I'd written and accepted that it wasn't going to be easy to get started without any input from forensics.

It was the Serendipity Social Committee, however, who initiated a surprising move that would enable me to study my fellow residents and detect any attitudes that weren't entirely devastated by Jane's death. The Social Committee left the following flyer in all our letter boxes.

SERENDIPITY WAKE.

We on the Social Committee are deeply saddened and shocked by Jane Gasper's murder. We invite all residents to meet in the Restaurant each day at 10am for morning tea until Jane's body is released for burial and the funeral to celebrate her life has been conducted.

We need to support each other in our grief; we need to remember the vibrant life of our dear friend; we need to be there to support Ray in his shattering grief.

We hope and pray that this Serendipity Wake will help us all through the difficult days ahead.

I took the flyer across to Jean who'd already collected her own from her letterbox.

'This is a very perceptive idea that the social committee has come up with,' I said. 'It goes well beyond their usual diet of bus trips and concerts.'

'Yes, 'Jean replied. 'I've been thinking about it, I wonder if the suggestion came from Rachael, She must have hated the schism in the village that required her to get the police in to protect me from those vigilantes. This wake could be just what's needed to bring people together again.'

'you could be right, but full marks to the Social Committee for acting on the suggestion whoever it came from, particularly when one of the vigilantes is on that Social Committee.

'I'd say that the full marks must go to Rachael if she's been able to convince the committee to over-ride Martha Setright,' Jean said.

'So you'll come to the Wake with me,' I said.

'No, I won't risk any tentative moves to restore peace by being there. I'll come to the funeral, but not the Wake.'

Jean was right to stay away. It would have been difficult for her to ignore the animosity of all those in the village who believed that Barnaby stabbed

Jane Gasper and impossible for her to prevent Martha Setright from giving voice to her warped conclusions no matter how inappropriate the occasion. I would miss her though. Her sharp observations of people would have been useful to me as I studied the gathering for signs that someone may have information about the murder that they were taking pains to keep to themselves.

The Wake was well attended and the restaurant gradually filled up with people gravitating to the groups that formed naturally at any social function. The indoor bowlers sat together, as did the craft people, and the ukulele players and the ladies who formed their friendships in the exercise classes. All found their places to produce a gathering that was normal for the Village.

I couldn't be critical of this tendency for friendships to be dictated by common interests because I made my way immediately to the table made up of philosophy club members and the avid book readers. One group, however, was newly formed, drawing its numbers from various groups. They were now recognized as the Serendipity Vigilantes. I wasn't surprised to see them together and I didn't disapprove of their presence. They obviously weren't there to protest against Jean being allowed to stay on in the village. They were there to support Ray and surround him with their affection and concern. I looked at Ray as I passed their table and I didn't see the Ray we'd all become used to. He was quiet and subdued and he was tired and his eyes were red. He had lost his partner in a brutal stabbing and he needed and deserved unequivocal empathy from us all.

The people at my table were all used to talking with each other and the conversation flowed smoothly as concerns were expressed for Ray's future without Jane, and then someone mentioned that we should establish some sort of memorial in the village to honour Jane who had died so young a few months before her seventieth birthday. That got a discussion going and we were well into our delicious sultana scones and some were pouring their second cup of tea before Lilian Kershaw, who coordinated the book club, started a different conversation.

She told how she'd woken from a dream on the morning of the murder and in the dream, she'd gone to a fashion parade where Jane Gasper was one of the models. She'd been so real in the dream, but she must have been dead by then. She walked along the catwalk wearing some sort of indescribable robe and I watched her until she disappeared through the curtain at the end of the platform.

Everyone responded to Lillian's story and everyone recognized how chilling it would have been to wake up and find that someone you'd been dreaming about had been murdered, but no one tried to interpret the dream. However, Annabel Plunket, a member of the Philosophy Club gave another dimension to it when she told of an experience she'd had on the morning of the murder.

She was up early because she had an 8.30 am dental appointment at the Teachers' Health Clinic on St Pauls Terrace. At 9.30 it was all done except for one very numb mouth. She headed off down into Fortitude Valley to reward the rest of her body with a cup of tea and a piece of the most decadent cake she could find.

She had just about reached the Brunswick Street Food Court when she noticed a man hurrying along the footpath on the other side of the street. There were other people over there, but she noticed this man because she thought he was Ray Gasper. He disappeared into one of the dark doorways that she'd always assumed gave entrance to one of the dens of vice that had changed the character of the Valley since the Department Stores closed their doors. She worried about Ray getting mixed up in that sort of thing until she got back to Serendipity and the news of Jane's murder erased all other worries from her mind. The thought of Ray learning of his wife's murder when he rang from Sydney was such a poignant thing to have happened that she forgot all about her little mistaken identity incident in Brunswick street until Lillian told everyone about her dream.

Not necessarily mistaken identity,' Roger Masters said. 'What you were seeing, Annabel, could have been a phantasm, A spirit, Ray Gasper's demented spirit in this case. It appeared to you at the time of Ray's phone call that delivered to him the devastating news of Jane's murder.'

'You've lost the plot this time, Roger,' Lillian Kershaw said. 'Ray Gasper was down in Sydney. What was his spirit, demented or otherwise doing up here in Fortitude Valley?'

'A spirit is not governed by the laws of the physical universe. It doesn't occupy space, and time needed to traverse space is irrelevant. You yourself, Lillian, glimpsed Jane's departing spirit at the moment of her murder and you didn't need to be out in the park, and Annabel wasn't down in Sydney to witness Ray Gasper's agitated spirit disappearing into the darkness as he made his phone call.'

That's all a bit far-fetched, Roger,' Lillian said. 'I'll stick to the verdict of mistaken identity to explain what Annabel saw because anything else is outside life as we know it.'

'And you'll ignore the strange coincidence of what both Annabel and Lillian experienced. I'll have to have a session on phantasms and poltergeists, and out of body experiences in our philosophy club. It's up to the philosophers to deal with the para-normal because scientists are trapped in the physical universe blinkered by what you call life as we know it.'

'Here, here,' one of the book club members said, 'I'll come to that session. I'm really hooked on science fiction.'

A metaphysical discussion got going then and I took the opportunity to observe other groups in the room, but I didn't notice anything untoward in appearances or behaviour. I had about two weeks at my disposal because while the body was released for burial after one week, the funeral was another week away to give some overseas mourners time to arrive. My only certainty after two weeks of joining different tables to observe people and talk to them was that no one at the extended wake was guilty of the murder. I was a little curious, however, about who was coming from overseas because neither Jane nor Ray seemed to have any living relatives in Australia.

Chapter 19

The day of the funeral arrived with sunshine and a gentle autumn breeze providing for the comfort of those who were out and about, and that included most of the residents of Serendipity Village on this day. Those with cars pooled them to transport residents without cars and Serendipity management provided a special bus to take those who couldn't get a seat in a car. Nobody who wanted to bid farewell to one of the most respected Serendipity residents was going to be left behind.

Jean and I drove down early to the Crematorium at Albany Creek so that I could check on the chapel and select a seat that would enable me to have a good view of the mourners in the front pews. I wasn't some sort of voyeur getting gratification from the private grief of others. I was a working policeman with a murder to solve and I didn't intend letting any opportunity slip by to monitor behaviour that might suggest that someone was experiencing any emotion other than genuine grief. I'd taken a fortnight to rule out that any Serendipity resident was a suspect. I'd have one hour now to either eliminate mourners from outside the Village or single out one for further attention.

As the mourners from the village arrived, they glanced at the hearse ready there with the coffin and they looked away overcome by some vision of Jane Gasper confined in its dark interior never to be released. They concentrated on getting themselves into one of the two queues that formed for the signing of the condolence record watched over by sombre gentlemen from the Undertaker's Parlour.

Ray Gasper arrived surrounded by his close friends from the village. A pathway was opened up for them and they went straight in to occupy the two rows at the front on the left-hand side. The Anglican priest joined them there to offer Ray words of comfort before he conducted the service to celebrate Jane's life.

I was half turned in my seat so I could see when Rachael arrived and I waved to her to join Jean and me. She'd obviously left Serendipity after the last of the residents had set off for the funeral and probably after she'd had a final check of the auditorium to see that it was properly prepared for the morning tea we'd be having after we'd all said our farewells to Jane.

Five minutes before the service was due to start, a group of six arrived. I watched them walk down the aisle and take their place in the front pews on the right-hand side. The priest came over and shook hands with each one of them. Obviously, they had some association with the deceased although none of the people around Ray Gasper seemed to know them and Ray himself gave them a look that suggested that he didn't welcome their presence.

'I wonder who they are,' I said to Rachael.

'I know two of them,' she replied. 'The tall one is Roland Haywell, Jane's financial adviser and the older man is Fred Walla her accountant.'

'She has both a financial adviser and an accountant? Most self-funded retirees get by with a financial adviser. There must have been a fair amount of money involved for her to have needed both.'

'I don't know what her circumstances were, but that's how Jane introduced them to me when we met at a function last year. Both Haywell and Walla belong to the same firm.'

'I take it that the women with them are their wives.'

'I've never met their wives, but I'd say you're right which probably means that Jane was more than just a client of the firm if wives come to the funeral.'

'That's what I was thinking. I wonder if that same closeness extends to the other two in the party. They're African, aren't they?'

'Yes,' Jean said joining our conversation. 'I'd put them down as African and I'd also classify them as husband and wife. I've been watching their interaction with other.'

'Thank you, Jean, for noticing that. I've been too busy looking at the others,'

'I wonder if their getting here was the reason for delaying the funeral,' Rachael said.

'Rachael,' I said, 'will you do something for me? When we go back to the Village for the morning tea Serendipity is so generously providing, I want you to renew your acquaintance with Haywell and Walla and find out who the Africans are and what their connection is to Jane Gasper, and if you can you might suss out Jane's financial position. Where there's money there is a motive for murder. I don't think husband, Ray, is too happy with his wife's finance team. We might have to end up sending the police auditors in.'

Our conversation ended abruptly when the priest approached the lectern and got the service underway. It proceeded along predictable lines with readings of passages from the bible that focus on death, the singing of the 23rd psalm and a short sermon about the meaning of life, but I was disappointed when the priest went on to deliver the eulogy as well. He obviously didn't know Jane and he was putting together some notes he'd been given. I and I'm sure most of the others there couldn't help thinking that Jane Gasper was absent from her own funeral.

My apologies to the priest because he had something so extraordinary lined up for us that we had to accept the obvious truth that none of us had ever known who Jane Gasper really was, not even Ray I suspect who had come to his marriage with her later in his life. We didn't know what was coming when the priest called on the African lady, Weizero Yenu, to continue the eulogy with her revelation of a Jane Gasper that none of us knew. Yenu took her place at the lectern and spoke with clarity and assurance.

I'm Yenu and my husband, who's also here today, is called Caleb. We've come from Ethiopia with heavy hearts to mourn with you the death of Jane Gasper. Jane

Gasper was one of God's angels whose time on earth was a blessing and a channel of grace for my people in the town of Moyale in Ethiopia.

'I met Jane in 1975, twenty-five years ago. That was the only time I've seen her face to face as she spent that wonderful fortnight with me. It was a bad time for Moyale split on the border between Ethiopia and Kenya. It was a time of terrorism, government corruption and neglect, and a time when people were going hungry because of the drought.

'I was depressed because I had a dream that had no chance of coming to fruition. My dream was to see a school established in the Ethiopian part of Moyale. We had no schools and to get an education children had to cross over into the Kenyan part of the town and suffer the discrimination that was rife there.

'Jane rejected outright any conclusion that my dream couldn't be achieved. She said that if I could get together a committee of competent people who dreamed the dream that I dreamed, she would be able to find the money. Two months after she left, the money arrived, all of it, and the building of our school was underway.

'At first, I didn't believe that the money had come from Jane Winslow as she was then. It came from the TAWA foundation and her signature wasn't on the documents. I wanted to shout from the rooftops about the generosity of this TAWA foundation and I emailed back for information about it. The reply came immediately. TAWA means To Africa With Affection and TAWA is a foundation established by Ms Jane Winslow.'

Weizero Yenu went on to tell about other TAWA projects including one that lavished affection on the Afar tribe from the Horn of Africa. The Afars were a proud and independent race who lived a nomadic life moving from well to well grazing their animals. They were a minority group, however, and they were ignored by government when their wells started to dry up. Caleb was an Afar tribesman and he came south in a desperate bid to rescue his people from certain death. Yenu's story had a happy ending. TAWA money dug new wells right across Afar territory and Yenu said yes to Caleb's marriage proposal.

By the time Yenu finished her eulogy to Jane Gasper, I'm sure I wasn't the only one in the chapel to be enthralled by the massive amounts of money she must have outlaid. Her life was so sadly cut short while she was living in modest accommodation in a retirement village. Where did all her money come from?

I turned to Rachael as the front pews started to file out when Jane's coffin was no longer with us.

'What we know now poses more questions than are answered by what we've just been told. Where did the money come from? Was money a motive for the murder? How much did Ray know about all this? What was behind his dark looks when the money people arrived? And what about his reaction to Yenu? Did you notice that?

'Yes. I couldn't work out whether he really was a stunned mullet or whether he was just pretending to be one.'

'Good, you've got the picture. I'll be waiting with keen anticipation for what you glean from your conversations with Haywell and Walla, and Yenu and Caleb as well although Yenu has probably told us everything she knows about what happened to the money in Africa. I want a light shone on the source of the money.

'I'll do my best,' Rachael said after a little hesitation.'

'I'm sorry, Rachael, I got carried away. I sound like a chief Inspector allocating duties for the day. I'm a little frustrated with my undercover status which doesn't allow me much room to question anybody myself.'

'No, no, Frank, I didn't hesitate because I was reluctant to continue being involved in the investigation. I was just thinking that Haywell and Walla probably won't discuss a client's business with me just as I would not talk about the private lives of the Residents at Serendipity, but nevertheless I will take them into the privacy of my office and give them every opportunity to sing the praises of this remarkable woman.'

Rachael joined the line making its slow progress through the front door of the chapel and I turned to Jean to apologise for neglecting her during the service, and then turning to Rachael immediately after it. About fifteen minutes later we were driving back to Serendipity to join the rest of the residents in a morning tea that was more than equal to the task of providing our lunch as well.

Chapter 20

I knocked on Rachael's back door at about 4 o'clock on the day of the funeral. Rachael knew who it was and called me in.

'I was about to ring you,' she said. 'Haywell and Walla were happy to talk and I've got plenty to tell you.'

'You know where the money came from then.'

'Yes. She bought a golden casket ticket twenty years ago and she won 15 million

'What!'

'Yes, she won 15 million and she took a trip to Africa to look for projects that she could give financial support to.'

'What an extraordinary thing to do with 15 million.'

'She was an extraordinary woman. Far from shouting her good fortune from the roof tops, she recognized the pressure she'd be subjected to from people begging her to distribute the money to support all their own selfish schemes.'

'She must have had family or relatives who would have appreciated a helping hand. Why did she go to Africa?'

'She had no living relatives. She was completely alone in the world so she went to Fred Walla for advice. She knew him and she knew he could be trusted to keep the business confidential. Fred Walla had recently joined with Roland Haywell to establish the finance firm of Haywell and Walla.'

'She did the right thing in seeking professional advice, but I wonder how sound their advice was.'

'I think it was very sound. Fred Walla managed to satisfy her desire to use her money to help people in real need.'

'There's nothing wrong with that as long as her own need for a comfortable life and adequate superannuation wasn't neglected.'

'It wasn't. Fred advised her to invest $1million of her windfall in an annuity to give her an income for life and he suggested that the remainder could be deposited in a charity trust fund that his firm could administer for her when she decided what project she wanted to support. It was Fred who suggested that she resign from her Public Service job and take a trip around Australia or overseas to find some cause that she really wanted to support. As you now know she went to Africa and she called her charity foundation TAWA.'

'That brings us to the $14million question. Did Ray Gasper know about his wife's philanthropy?'

'No he didn't, not until the funeral. He really was a stunned mullet this morning.'

'It's unbelievable that such wealth was kept secret from him.'

'Haywell and Walla made sure that all TAWA business was quarantined in their office. Nothing went to her personally after she married Ray. They judged that the husband she'd chosen was more interested in her $1million investment than he was in her. They were right. He kept demanding money for impossible schemes he dreamed up and she was inclined to give in to him. They were determined to avoid the pressure he'd bring to bear if he knew that she had 14 million to dip into.'

'What happens now? Did Jane Gasper leave a will?'

'Yes, she did. Whatever money she has in her annuity will go to Ray and Haywell and Walla will be letting him know that they have no further interest in managing that investment. They think he'll go through the money and he'll end up on the age pension, but it won't be any concern of theirs.'

Will there be anything in the will about the future of TAWA?'

'Right from the beginning fiduciary arrangements were in place for the fund to be administered independently, without Jane's involvement apart from advice about beneficiaries. There's no sunset clause so Haywell and Walla or their successors will continue to administer the charity in perpetuity.'

'And that arrangement is endorsed in Jane's will?'

'Yes, except that Haywell and Walla will be required to establish a committee to select beneficiaries according to guidelines that are stipulated.'

'Has the will been read already?'

'No, next Wednesday is set down for that.'

'They seem to know what's in it.'

'Yes, that's because the will was drawn up by the firm's solicitor when the TAWA foundation was established.'

'Haywell and Walla have the TAWA foundation tied up as tight as a Gordian knot which seems to me to be a little unfair to Ray Gasper. I don't particularly like the man because normally he's a loudmouth, but Jane's death has quietened him down. He could have been given some role in TAWA as it continues on as a magnificent memorial to his wife.'

Rachael didn't agree with me, nor did Jean when I asked her about it. They both pointed out that Jane Gasper would have known what her husband was like. She had plenty of opportunity to change the will after she married him, but she didn't do that. Jean in particular rejected any suggestion that Jane was a vacillating and unassertive woman dominated by her accountant.

I am not sure that Ray can be legally excluded from the operation of his wife's charity foundation as Haywell have set out to do, but whether or not he deserves a role in it is not germane to my search for a murderer. Neither Ray nor Fred Walla appear to fit the role of the murderer. At the time of Jane's murder Fred Walla had the confidence of his client and the , management of TAWA had never been questioned. As for Ray, he appeared to get on well with his wife who seemed willing to provide for whatever needs he had. He had no knowledge that his wife was a rich woman who had surrendered her wealth to philanthropy so there is no motive for him to scheme to acquire the unknown wealth for himself.

The day after the reading of the will, however, I had to modify that assessment of Ray when Roger Masters dropped in to let me know what was happening in the auditorium.

'Ray Gasper is down there,' he said 'and he's ranting and raving to anyone who'll listen telling them in his stentorian voice that the finance firm of Haywell and Walla had stolen Jane's charity foundation, the whole 14 million of it.'

'14 million!' I said pretending surprise. There's been plenty of speculation about the size of the fund since the funeral, but none of the rumours had it at 14 million. I can't believe, though that Haywell and Walla are ripping it off.'

'It stunned everyone that such a huge amount could be stolen,' Roger Masters said, 'so I appointed myself as a spokesman for the group and I said to Ray that everyone was as astonished as he was when that woman said that his wife spent all that money in Africa, but to find out now that all his wife's money had been stolen by Haywell and Walla beggared belief. Ray then said that he'd always known about TAWA, but what astonished him at the funeral was that the African woman was talking about it. He said that neither he nor Jane had ever given permission for their Charity to be made public and linked to them.'

I said to Roger that it would have been unconscionable to make public what he and Jane wanted to keep private if that is what happened, but it wouldn't amount to theft. Police will be auditing TAWA books if a complaint is made that money has disappeared.

Roger said that a police audit of the books wasn't going to satisfy Ray. He is announcing to all and sundry that the wrong will was read. It was twenty years old. The new will, drawn-up after the marriage, is the only relevant will and he'd be seeing Haywell and Walla in court.

I thanked Roger for filling me in on what was going on and he left with a reminder to me that the monthly meeting of the philosophy club was due on Friday to which I replied, 'What could possibly cause me to miss a meeting of the philosophy club?'

I retired to my squatters chair on the back patio to consider the new possibilities that Roger's news had opened up. Haywell and Walla could run a bent firm and they've organized Jane's murder to give them access to the 14 million that is willed to them in a document they drew up twenty years earlier and Ray also becomes a suspect because he claims to have known about his wife's $14million no doubt to boost the assumption that it will pass on to him when a more recent will is found. I realize that Ray would be less of a suspect if he didn't know about the $14million but he would have known about the $800,000 annuity that provided their income. How desperate was he for money?

Sweetman is confident that he already has the killer in custody, but I am equally confident that he hasn't. I will be treading on his toes, but I must talk to him about a full audit of the TAWA books, the legitimacy of the will that virtually transferred control of TAWA funds to Haywell and Walla, and the removal of Ray Gasper from any association with the fund which Ray claims was a joint interest for both himself and his wife after he married her.

Chapter 21

I went to sleep again with my conscious mind full of suspects this time. Some of them were unlikely ones, who'd drifted into my thinking uninvited. Fred Walla was there and Ray Gasper of course, but also a certain cleaner from the shopping centre and Mark Dollinger our maintenance man whom I once suspected of theft, and as well I dreamed up images of deranged men who, coming across a lone female in a deserted park as night fell, took the opportunity to rob her of her life.

The human brain, however, doesn't shut down when its body is asleep. It has a subconscious department that works the night shift on a problem when the conscious mind is out of action. Thus I was presented with a solution to one of my problems as soon as I woke. I was astonished that I'd overlooked something that was so obvious. I'd spent time bemoaning my exclusion from the crime scene and never once gave any thought to a part of that scene that was available to me and carried the potential to identify the murderer.

Breakfast was a celebration as I devoured my weet-bix and pondered the two suspects for whom $14million was a motive for murder. The one in the village might well be shown to be linked to the crime if I could get hold of his shoes. I left for the Roma Street police precinct fully confident that I'd be reporting a breakthrough Chief Inspector Sweetman couldn't ignore.

'Chief Inspector Sweetman is not available,' the receptionist said when I asked if I could see him.

'I'll wait until he is available,' I replied. 'How long do you expect him to be?'

'I've no idea the girl said. The assistant Commissioner has called him in for a conference. It could take until lunch time.'

'Could you leave a note on his desk to let him know I'll be back at lunch time and I'll bring my own sandwiches. It's quite urgent that I talk to him.'

'You can't come barging in off the street and demand an interview with a chief inspector. I can organize a sergeant to listen to what you have to say and there won't be any delay for you. What's your name?'

'Frank Coleman,' I said, but I added, 'DCI Sweetman will want to talk to me personally.'

Her eyes widened as she gave me a penetrating look. 'Well that's the strangest coincidence,' she said, 'The Deputy Commissioner wants to talk to you as well. He asked me to contact you and I've been ringing, but you're not at home obviously. I'd have done better to call out across the counter, are you there Mr Coleman?'

Her tone had changed suddenly from its reprimanding mode to accommodate her bright and cheery repartee, but I didn't feel like being cheery. I was deflated. I knew why he wanted to see me. He wanted to terminate my services at the Village. Sweetman had convinced him that I was now surplus to requirements. I'd come in to report a break through and plan the next move, but I was going to be shown the door.

'You're to go straight in,' the receptionist said as she switched off the intercom after reporting my arrival.

'Frank Coleman,' Assistant Commissioner Baxter said when I entered his office, 'Thank you for responding so quickly to my summons. We have a problem that you might be able to help us with.'

I relaxed. My services weren't going to be terminated. 'I'll be happy to help in any way I can,' I said.

'Good. DCI Sweetman gave you the job of transferring Barnaby Reid from a police cell to a hospital ward and I understand that you and Reid's aunt are still good neighbours.' 'Yes,' I said flatly as I wondered what my private life had to do with the problem that he was seeking my help with.

'The psychiatrist treating Barnaby Reid has requested that the charge against him be dropped so he can be transferred to a private clinic in Victoria. He's made his request through political channels and the police minister has asked the Commissioner for a full report on the case.'

I couldn't have been more delighted that such a request was being considered at the highest level, but I knew that I'd have to be circumspect with my words. I'd need the full co-operation of DCI Sweetman to bring the real murderer to justice.

'Did the psychiatrist give a reason for his obvious presumption of Barnaby Reid's innocence?' I said.

'Not really,' the Deputy Commissioner replied. 'He presumed him innocent because the recorded history of his recently diagnosed bi-polar disease didn't suggest violence at any stage. He was concerned that his patient appeared to be traumatised by his arrest and he was refusing to talk to anyone. He wants to remove him completely from any police environment even though the police are not in evidence in the psychiatric ward.'

I knew that the cause of Barnaby's silence went beyond his arrest, but I wasn't at liberty to say how I knew that. I was sure, however, that Jean would be prepared to talk to someone like the Deputy Commissioner in the strictest confidence. Having all charges dropped and Barnaby removed completely from the shadow of her book and its underground bunker would be her number one priority.

'Barnaby's aunt knows that her nephew is no murderer,' I said, 'but her hands are tied when it comes to explaining his behaviour when he was being investigated for theft. That behaviour may well put him in the running for a murder charge in police thinking and I'm sure his Aunt would welcome a confidential talk with you, Assistant Commissioner, to put you in the picture.'

'I don't like the sound of that,' DCI Sweetman said. 'No amount of confidential information can alter the fact that the murder weapon was found in Reid's knapsack.'

'Were his finger prints found on the handle of the knife,' I said.

'No, he'd wiped the handle clean, but the blood on the blade was the victim's blood and the knife was in his possession. You yourself agreed that his arrest was our only option.'

'Don't worry about anything that the aunt might be planning to pass on to me, DCI Sweetman,' the Assistant Commissioner said. 'I'll be making it a condition of my interview with her that I'll be discussing anything she says to me with the officer heading the investigation.'

'I'm sure she'll agree to that.' I said. 'She won't be talking about any criminal activity she's attempting to have swept under the carpet. It'll be more about an every-day, above board, but sensitive commercial contract.'

DCI Sweetman, still confident that Barnaby was guilty continued to press his judgement, 'You seem to be well versed in the lady's affairs, Inspector Coleman. You would do well to take advantage of your relationship with her to prepare her for her nephew's conviction for a crime that he committed while he wasn't of sound mind.'

'My relationship, as you call it, is that of a good neighbour who's there to help in time of trouble so you need have no worries about me preparing her for impending disaster should it become necessary.'

'Glad to hear that, Frank,' the Assistant Commissioner said. 'I've been discussing the case with DCI Sweetman and since there is only one suspect and he had the murder weapon in his possession and he's also of unsound mind, there's a more than even chance that the poor fellow is guilty and his aunt will need to come to terms with that.'

'I'd agree with that if there was only one suspect, but I came here this morning to report to DCI Sweetman that a breakthrough has emerged. I have two more suspects who need to be investigated.'

'What! Trust you Inspector Coleman to obstruct the smooth course of Justice with wagon loads of suspects.'

'Only two,' I said.

'Two or twenty-two, they've all got to be assessed no matter how unlikely they are. When we've finished here, we'd better go back to my office and sort them out.'

'No,' the Assistant Commissioner intervened. 'You can do that here. I want to be in on this, it may be relevant to the report I have to write for the pollies.'

Chapter 22

ssistant Commissioner Baxter called for tea and biscuits and we settled down to pursue the course of justice. There was no more talk of obstructing it once I got into my summary of Yenu Weizero's eulogy for Jane Gasper and moved from there to the information Rachael Parker was able to get from Fred Walla about keeping the existence of the TAWA Foundation a secret from Ray Gasper and ended up with Roger Master's report on Ray Gasper's extreme behaviour in the auditorium.

'I find it difficult to believe that Fred Walla is engaged in any deception with a $14million trust he's administering. He's a fellow Rotarian of mine and he's a tireless worker for the club,' the Assistant Commissioner said.

'Nevertheless an accusation has been made that he's channelling money into his own coffers,' DCI Sweetman responded, 'and he admits that he tried to keep the very existence of the fund well hidden from Ray Gasper. Unfortunately for Walla there were, apparently, no secrets between Gasper and his wife.'

'Yes, it doesn't look good for Fred and, heaven forbid, if he did have Jane Gasper removed from the scene, her husband's outburst is more than warranted. Never the less, DCI Sweetman, if I were you, I wouldn't charge in with the police auditors until you've interviewed Ray Gasper and established that his accusation is more than a wild assumption,'

It was time for me to add my opinion to the discussion I'd started.

'Ray Gasper needs to be questioned on more than the accusation he's made about Fred Walla. Remember that all the money belonged to his wife so he had exactly the same motive to get rid of her as Fred Walla had.

'I wouldn't agree with that,' DCI Sweetman said. 'According to what you saw of his reaction at the funeral and what Walla himself said, he didn't know about the $14million.'

'I still don't think he knew about it,' I said. 'He's only claiming that he did now to add credibility to his claim that it was being stolen by Walla. What he did know about was the $800,000 in his wife's bank account and since he was in urgent need of money and Walla was advising his wife not to hand over the $200,000, he was asking for, he did what he had to do to get hold of it in her will.'

You're using a long bow to reach that verdict, and you accuse me of jumping to conclusions. I find the murder weapon in the possession of a likely killer and you want the charge dropped, but here you are suggesting that a man murdered his wife whom he got on well with because he needed some money. He must have been desperate for that money.'

'I think he was. On the morning of the murder, one of our Serendipity residents thought she saw him disappearing into a building of ill repute in Fortitude Valley. He was supposed to have been in Sydney.'

'That puts him close to the murder scene,' DCI Sweetman said. 'Have you followed up on what the resident saw?'

'I have, but the resident is convinced now that it was a case of mistaken identity on her part. Like everyone else she's traumatised by Gasper's tragic call from Sydney on that morning. Telstra wasn't much help in identifying where that Sydney call really came from.'

'The sooner they get around to keeping a record of all communication data the better,' DCI Sweetman said.

'That will come when government decides that it needs to keep track of terrorists talking to each other. Privacy won't be an issue then,' Assistant Commissioner said.

I had my opinion about any authority recording private phone calls, but now wasn't the time to get into that discussion. I hadn't yet revealed how certain I was that I could change a mere suspect into a proven culprit.

'The reason I mentioned that sighting in the Valley was to draw attention to the building Ray Gasper, or the man he was mistaken for, was seen to enter. It's the one almost opposite the railway station and it's a den of vice according to the people I talked to, with gambling big time, sex, drugs, the lot. If Ray Gasper lost money in there, he'd be lent on heavily to pay up. He might even be driven to murder to get money together.'

'That would seem to settle it then. You've established that Ray Gasper needs investigating as your number one suspect,' the Assistant Commissioner said.

'All right! All right,' DCI Sweetman said holding up his hands in mock capitulation. Slowly, slowly catchee monkey. The pollies can have a win and Barnaby Reid can go off to the comfort of Victoria while we turn our attention to the Gasper man.'

'I wouldn't rush in to releasing Barnaby Reid,' the Assistant Commissioner said, 'He's the only one you have any evidence against. All you have against Gasper at the moment is a motive all be it a plausible one, but juries don't convict on motives no matter how plausible they are.'

'If Ray Gasper is our murderer,' I said, 'he will supply us with all the evidence we need.'

'If Ray Gasper is the murderer, he's more likely to take pains to deny us any evidence,' DCI Sweetman said.

'True,' I said, but he doesn't know he's harbouring the evidence I'm thinking of.'

Sweetman and the Assistant Commissioner both looked at me as I savoured the little triumph of my breakthrough.

'You'd better tell about the evidence you're thinking of so we can all think about it,' the Assistant Commissioner said,'

'It won't need any thought,' I said. 'If it's there it's there. A couple of days before the murder, Jean Reid decided to do something about the ants that were taking over her back patio. She used a product that had been produced by an industrial chemist friend of hers in Victoria. It wasn't on the market here in Australia. It looked like sawdust, but it was lethal to ants. The modus operandi was to leave it sprinkled around for two or three days so the ants could carry it back to the nest for a maximum kill. It was still sprinkled around on the morning of the murder.'

'Eureka!' DCI Sweetman exclaimed. 'If Gasper has any of that unique ant killer in the treads of his sneakers or whatever shoes he was wearing that morning he could only have picked it up from that patio as he walked across to drop the murder weapon into Barnaby Reid's knapsack.'

The Assistant Commissioner just smiled, but I think his smile was as much about Sweetman's sudden turnaround in relation to Barnaby's guilt as it was about the happy progress of the case.

'Getting hold of his shoes could be a problem,' I said. 'It would need to be done without alerting him about why we wanted them.'

'You're the undercover man in the Village. That will be your job. I'll make it easy for you though. I'll take Gasper into Roma Street for questioning about his claim that Haywell and Walla have been misappropriating money from the TAWA Trust. The sun will be setting when I cart him off so you'll have the cover of darkness to hide your operation.'

'I'm impressed by your ability to think on your feet and steer the operation in another direction as required. Perhaps you might have a suggestion about getting hold of the key to Gasper's unit. The Village manager cooperates well with the police, but it's a mantra for her that nobody enters a dwelling without the permission of the resident.'

'You'll have to use your excellent powers of persuasion then. However you do that is up to you. I never interfere with the operational tactics of an undercover agent.'

'Thanks very much,' I said. 'I don't know what tactic you're suggesting, but I certainly won't be putting Rachael in any compromising position to get her cooperation.

Assistant Commissioner Baxter terminated any further discussion of undercover tactics by turning the focus back onto DCI Sweetman's role.

'You may not interfere with the tactics of an undercover agent, but I sometimes interfere with the course of an investigation by making suggestions. Have you given any thought to what happens to your evidence when the ant killer on the soles of a shoe is reduced to circumstantial evidence by a smart barrister?'

'Yes, I have and my response will be that it's a unique ant killer that could only be found on the tiles of the one patio where the murder weapon was found,' DCI Sweetman said a little impatiently.'

'You are saying then that whoever waked on that patio over those two or three days should be charged with Jane Gasper's murder. That will include you yourself, Frank Coleman or any of the other neighbours who dropped in to see Jean Reid.'

'You are ignoring the fact that nobody else had the motive that Ray Gasper had.'

'And you are forgetting that a smart barrister will present Ray Gasper as a completely innocent man who dropped in on Barnaby before flying off to Sydney.'

I thought that the Assistant Commissioner was developing a highly unlikely scenario to devaluate the evidence I'd come up with and frustrate DCI Sweetman's enthusiasm to run with it.

'Ray Gasper had never gone and would not go to Jean Reid's unit on a social visit,' I said. 'If he has the ant killer on the soles of his shoes, it got there during a clandestine visit to drop a knife in Barnaby's knapsack.'

'You may know that for the truth, but Ray Gasper's barrister will be painting a picture of a man who is as pure as the driven snow. The police had dropped the charge against Barnaby and Ray had called in to congratulate him and apologise on behalf of the village for any hurt that may have been caused. It was just unfortunate that the Reids weren't home at the time or they didn't hear him knocking.'

'You're right Assistant Commissioner,' DCI Sweetman said. 'We'll have to have a completely watertight case if we charge him with murder. He'll have the prospect of getting his hands on 14 million so he won't have any trouble attracting the barrister he needs.'

'Good, I have every confidence that you'll come up with the watertight evidence we'll need to put him away.'

'Actually I have the germ of an idea already, but it will mean resorting to entrapment to get him. What's your attitude to the use of entrapment?'

'We use entrapment all the time. What is an undercover agent if he's not an entrapment agent?'

'Good, I'll get down to business,' DCI Sweetman said.

'Will my services be required in your business?' I said.

'Of course. Your first job is to get hold of those shoes. Once Forensics has identified the ant killer embedded in the soles, we'll organise the drama that will surround his arrest.'

Chapter 23

Getting hold of the shoes was not a problem after I'd surmounted the hurdle of getting hold of the key to Ray Gasper's place. Rachael wanted me to produce a warrant to search the unit with Ray in attendance. I had to convince her that we needed to do it without alerting him that he was a suspect. She held firm to her mantra that Serendipity was a place where the privacy of residents in their units was sacrosanct and she couldn't agree to any clandestine police intrusion. I exposed a chink in her defences, however, when I reminded her of Ray Gasper's attitude when she was organising the police search of the village after the sacking of the Monkton place. He'd stood up in the meeting she'd called and said that it made him mad as hell that police needed a search warrant to go after criminals and that it was pathetic that they had to ask permission to conduct a house-to-house search.

'Serendipity policy isn't there to counteract the rantings of people like Ray Gasper,' she responded.

'But what he said makes you wonder if he was expressing a firmly held belief or if his intention was to put himself in the police good books by supporting them with an extreme law and order view point.'

'You think he was building up Brownie points to protect him from police suspicion in the future?'

'I think he's cunning enough to look after his own interests no matter what they are. He'll have the money to employ a top barrister to protect him in the court if it comes to that so we don't want to give him the luxury of being able to plan his defences by alerting him that we suspect him before we can arrest him and lock him in a remand cell.'

'The last thing I want to do is to aid and abet Ray Gasper to escape a conviction if he's guilty, but I'm equally determined to uphold our privacy policy.'

'Could you entertain a compromise?' I said. 'Could you find some need to leave your office for a few moments?'

She looked at me and then she stood up. 'This is embarrassing,' she said. 'The scrambled eggs I had for breakfast have given me diarrhoea. I'll have to go. See yourself out.'

She was gone. I unlocked the key cabinet with the key she kept in her drawer, unhooked the master key and left by the back door.

As I said, getting the shoes was not a problem. I let myself into Ray Gasper's house after the sun went down and drew all the curtains before I turned on my powerful police torch.

In Ray's wardrobe I found a rack full of his shoes each pair of which I examined in turn. None of them appeared to have collected anything in the treads let alone ant killer. Then I noticed the two pair that had been pushed underneath the rack. The first pair I pulled out were obviously garden shoes with plenty of mud about them, but the second pair were the ones I'd been looking for. They were sneakers with their generous treads packed with what looked like sawdust.

First thing the next morning I got them to the forensics laboratory and then I dropped in on DCI Sweetman to make myself available for the next stage of the investigation whatever that might be.

'Did you get them?' he said as soon as I appeared in the doorway.

'Yes, I took them to forensics.'

'Good, the Assistant Commissioner has contacted Jean Reid and arranged the conference you suggested,'

'Will Jean be coming here?'

'No, no, she can't be seen anyway near Roma Street. He'll talk to her at the psychiatric ward.'

'Oh, but that might be handy, he could take the opportunity to talk to Barnaby with Jean there. He never clams up with Jean. I don't understand though why Jean can't be seen anyway near Roma Street.

'Because I don't want any rumour getting started that she's a police agent.'

'I don't follow, How could her entering a police precinct start a rumour that she's a police agent?'

'I'd better fill you in on how we plan to trap Ray Gasper into admitting that he murdered his wife. The entrapment involves a letter that we hope Jean Reid will be sending to Gasper. In the letter she asks him to meet her to discuss issues that are important to both of them. Obviously, there would be no meeting if Gasper picked up any gossip about Jean visiting a police station.'

'Have you taken leave of your senses! You must be floating in cloud cuckoo land if you think you can get away with arranging a meeting between an innocent member of the public and a suspected murderer even if there was no intention at all to badger him into a confession.'

'No, no, there will be no meeting at all between Jean Reid and Gasper, but there will be a well recorded meeting between Gasper and a policewoman who'll be impersonating Jean Reid. It will take place in the park in the semi dark and they'll be talking to each other from either end of the foot bridge across Cabbage Tree Creek. All that will be required of Jean Reid will be a letter in her own hand writing. We've already composed the letter. Here you'd better read it.'

I took the letter from him certain that Jean's involvement in the operation at any level was highly undesirable. DCI Sweetman hadn't thought it through. When I read it, I was more certain than ever that Jean would be putting herself at risk just by copying it out and signing it. This is what DCI Sweetman wanted her to copy and drop in Ray Gasper's letter box.

Dear Mr Gasper,

I'm well aware that we've never been friends, but I have a proposition to put to you which you'll find hard to ignore. I have evidence that puts you on my back patio on the morning of your wife's murder. You'll know why you were there. However, I myself have a certain need that you can fill and it will be no trouble for you to supply my need when you come into your full inheritance from your late wife.

You'll appreciate why I can't be specific about my evidence in this note, and you'll have no trouble in understanding that I'll have you over a barrel when my evidence puts you on my back veranda on the morning of your wife's murder.

Consequently, I'll expect to meet you on the footbridge in the park this Wednesday, 24th May at 6pm. I'll tell you then what it is that I have and you'll find out what you have to pay to get it back.

Please note that I will not have the evidence with me on Wednesday night nor do I keep it in my unit. It is held by a friend who will hand it straight to the police should you attempt to get hold of it prematurely.

As a further precaution against the violence towards me that you might be contemplating you will stay at the western end of the bridge (closest to the village) and I will move to the eastern end when I see you arrive.

Jean Reid.

'I can't be happy with this,' I said when I'd finished reading. 'On the surface it's a well-planned operation, but what about the repercussions against Jean when organized crime finds it's been denied a sizable slice of the 14 million that they are probably already planning to acquire for Gasper through the courts? Gasper will get nothing if he's in jail for murder and Jean will get a vindictive organized crime bullet for her part in putting him there.'

'The police won't back off putting a man in jail for fear of upsetting the crime bosses,' DCI Sweetman said.'

'And neither do they use members of the public as pawns to manoeuvre an arrest. I'm the undercover policeman and there's already a group in the village that think I was involved in the break-in there. A blackmail letter coming from me would almost be expected by Gasper. Jean can be left right out of it and you wouldn't even need to groom a police woman to do the confronting.'

'You can't leave Jean Reid right out of it. The murder weapon was deposited on her patio in her nephew's knapsack. Gasper has already killed one woman and another interfering woman might well stir him to use an uncontrollable flow of language that could see him convicted. Sorry Frank, we can't do without a Jean Reid lookalike.'

'You might feel justified in using a police woman as bait, but you are also involving an innocent member of the public. I'll be advising Jean not to write the letter.'

'Your advice will be a little late. The Assistant Commissioner is already at the hospital and Jean Reid will be writing the entrapment letter right now.'

I was appalled. It was nothing short of blackmail. Jean would copy out a letter to set up the confrontation with Gasper and the Assistant Commissioner would see to the instant release of Barnaby. DCI Sweetman, however, rejected my accusation.

'Barnaby will be on his way to Victoria whether she writes the letter or refuses to write the letter. The Police Minister's request has been granted.

It was obvious that Sweetman would not be changing any of the arrangements he'd made, so I only had one option to protect Jean from any underworld repercussions. I would have to put myself instead of her in any line of fire. Working out how I could do that was my determined focus until a modus operandi gelled for me.

Chapter 24

I went for a long walk on the afternoon of Wednesday 4th. I crossed the foot bridge and the park on the other side and strolled down a street enjoying some of the colourful autumn gardens that graced the suburb outside Serendipity Village. Shadows were lengthening as I recrossed the park to get back to the bridge. It had been a long day for me and also for DCI Sweetman as he ensured that everything would be in place and working for the little drama that was to take place on the bridge at sunset.

The council workers with their trailer of pruned branches and gardening tools also had knapsack sprays to deal with noxious weeds, but it turned out that they weren't council workers. They were police technicians who needed a feral weed eradication cover to potter around the bridge to fix their powerful little transmitter in place.

The young couple, who pulled into the caravan park with their van in tow, were directed to a vacant spot down at the forest fence. The first thing they did when they pulled up was to set up an antenna which prompted one grey nomad to comment that young people these days were unreal and should have stayed at home if all they were going to do when they got there was watch TV. He would have been bowled over by the array of receiving and recording equipment inside the van.

DCI Sweetman had invited me to drop in on the young couple and stay with them for the performance on the bridge, but I declined and continued to distance myself from a police performance that would be putting Jean Reid in jeopardy.

Back at the bridge, I looked up towards the shopping centre and noticed the woman coming into the park. I couldn't see who it was at that distance, but as she came along the creek pathway, I could see that she was wearing one of Jean's dresses. It was the police woman impersonator coming to do her duty. She'd spent most of the day at Jean's place trying on dresses and aging her face with makeup and practicing to produce the rhythms and tones of Jean's voice.

I moved behind a bush to avoid being seen by her. But by the time she was about halfway along the creek I decided to take my position in the wings or to be more specific, underneath the bridge where I'd prepared a place with a cushion and a blanket.

The western sky was starting to decorate itself with strips of vermillion bunting in preparation for the ritual farewell to the sinking sun and it was time for the curtain to go up on the bridge performance.

A gateway in the Serendipity wall opened and Ray Gasper peeped through. Seeing no-one on stage he made his entrance and took up his position at the end of the bridge. The police woman moved to hers and the war of words began.

'What the bloody hell do you think you're doing,' Gasper shouted to the actor at the other end of the bridge. 'You know your cretin of a nephew murdered my wife. The bastard's been arrested.'

'For something he didn't do!' the ersatz Jean Reid shouted back. 'I've got all the evidence the police will need to lock you up for life.'

'The police would need to be as limp-brained as you are to take any notice of evidence that you've dreamed up. You should be hiding away in shame after what your bloody nephew did, but you're all over the place like a headless chook trying to shift the blame to me. You're pathetic.'

'No amount of badmouthing me and Barnaby will save you if the police get hold of what I've got.' It came from my patio where you left the knife

'What have you got? Something of mine that you've picked up and planted on your patio. Any barrister would take that sort of evidence and toss it right out of the court room.'

'It's not what you left behind, but what you took away that will cook your goose.'

'You really are mad as a hatter. You think branding me as a thief will prove that I murdered my own wife? You're madder than a bloody hatter if you think you can blackmail me with evidence like that. That malicious little note you wrote will go straight to my barrister.'

'You'll have to tell him that I have your sneakers and they have an ant insecticide embedded in their soles that you could have only picked up from my patio during the two days it was down and it's an insecticide that only I could be using up here because it was made up by a friend of mine in Victoria and it's not on the market.'

'You've got my sneakers!' Ray Gasper shouted. 'I'll be adding theft to attempted black-mail and I'll be taking the matter straight to the police. They'll charge you with doctoring my sneakers as well.'

Underneath the bridge I was thinking that Sweetman's carefully arranged confrontation was falling flat on its face. It didn't seem likely that he'd be getting a confession out of Gasper, but the police woman fired another shot to try to unnerve him.

'Before you go involving the police,' she said, 'you might think about why you are talking to a barrister about all this. The police don't seem to suspect you of any crime so why do you have a barrister lined up if it's not to protect you from the consequences of the crime you committed. You might have a solicitor, everyone has a solicitor, but a barrister?'

Good girl I said to myself. Now you're putting some real pressure on him. Ray Gasper, however, was so well briefed that he tossed the question aside with ease.

'You're just clutching at straws in a ridiculous attempt to blackmail me into paying you for something you've dreamed up to link me to the murder your deranged nephew committed. He murdered my wife for God's sake and he's been arrested. I don't need a barrister to see that he's locked up for life. I've engaged a barrister, however, because Haywell and Walla have stolen 14 million from me. The barrister told me to expect all sorts of accusations to discredit me, but I wasn't to let any of them worry me because he'll have no trouble dealing with them in Court. Your charming little letter will go in my barrister's rubbish bin.'

That was it. Ray Gasper was well ahead on points and I had no other option but to enter the ring and take over from the police woman. I levered myself up onto the bridge and stood up in front of her, startling her as she searched for a reply to Gasper's last statement.

'I'll take over now,' I said quietly. 'Don't be surprised by anything I'm going to say.' With that I turned and strode along the bridge towards Ray Gasper. I wanted to be closer to the hidden microphone that his voice was going into.

'Hold it, hold it, Ray,' I said holding up my hands to let him see that I didn't have a weapon. 'This little exchange is heading off in the wrong direction.'

'Huh! Frank Coleman's crawled out from under a stone. I might have guessed that you'd be there.'

'Yes, but I know you Ray better than you know me and it's time I introduced myself.'

'I know as much about you as I want to know, Coleman. You're as crooked as a Boa Constrictor escaping and now, you're trying to blackmail me.'

'You flatter me, Ray. It takes a crook to know a crook and you've labelled me very nicely. So far, I've always managed to escape the attention of the police because I've got a little gang over in the Caravan Park to carry out projects like the heist in Rosella Lane. The other night while you were out, I asked one of my crew to borrow your sneakers for me.'

'What do you want me to do, congratulate you?'

'No, I just want to let you know that I'm on your side, Ray, and I'm here to help you because you're going to need it.'

'My barrister will give me all the help I'll need.'

'Are you sure of that? I'm not because I know something that your barrister doesn't know yet. You'll have to tell him about the ant insecticide in the soles of your shoes, but you'll also have to tell him that there will be some parthenium weed seeds underneath the insecticide.'

'And you know that because you put it all there. My barrister will see that coming a mile off.'

'I didn't put it there. You got the seeds from the crime scene in the park. I know the weed was there in the park where Jean was killed because I went over there as soon as the police left to see if there was anything in it for me and I saw the parthenium infestation. You can be sure that the police forensics team noticed it because it would have been them who brought it to the attention of the council who acted swiftly to get rid of it. It's a highly noxious weed and there's not much of it around now because it's zapped as soon as it's recognized.'

'You think you're Sherlock Holms don't you, playing your ukulele and finding everything I've ever done in the soles of my boots. You're no Sherlock, You're just a hood who's trying to blackmail me. It's a public park and anyone who walks in it will pick up park stuff on their shoes. My barrister will deal with your dodgy evidence.'

I won't be taking you to Court, Ray. I'm just pointing out that your sneakers will put you at the crime scene and also on the patio where the murder weapon ended up. I'll grant you that the organised crime bosses are good, I've used one myself on occasion. Your barrister will probably get you off the murder charge if it should come to that, but mud will stick and he'll find it nigh on impossible to get you custody of your 14 million. That will stay with the charity your wife founded and put in the hands of Haywell and Walla to administer. As far as the community is concerned your wife is unimpeachable and what she did is sacrosanct.'

My awarding of a badge of high community praise to his wife filled him with revulsion that he found difficult to suppress. He spoke in a quiet voice, but I'm sure that it wasn't too quiet for the transmitter to pick up.

'The selfish bitch was sitting on 14 million and she denied me the trifle that I asked for. She asked to be wasted and I gave her what she asked for.'

At last a clear admission of murder! I kept the conversation going though just in case DCI Sweetman needed an even clearer admission of guilt.

'And that should have been the end of it, Ray, you killed her and there shouldn't be any evidence linking you to the crime left lying around. I'll give your sneakers back to you and you'll put $300,000 into Jean's bank account. Jean has accepted that Barnaby will never have a normal life because of his bipolar. He'll beat the murder charge with a diminished responsibility plea, but she'll need $300,000 to set him up in a place where he'll be looked after.'

'The blackmailer wins,' Gasper said.

'Don't look on it as blackmail, Ray, it's just a necessary payment you need to make to get hold of your 14 million. You said $200,000 was a trifle when you asked your wife for it.'

Having to ask my wife if I could spend our money was the intolerable position Haywell and Walla put me in. When I'm in charge of allocating money from our charity none of it will go to blackmailers like you Coleman. Your extortion only works now because you threaten to muddy the court process to deny me my inheritance.

'You flatter me, Ray. Might I suggest that we meet in the Restaurant next Saturday for the transfer of the $300,000. Jean and I will invite you to lunch with us. It will be seen as a reconciliation gesture on our part and a recognition by you that Jean is not responsible for what Barnaby did.'

'Meeting in the Restaurant would be stupid. It's far too public for transferring money.'

'What do we have to hide? We'll be giving you what will look like a present in a box. You'll be giving me an envelope with a bank cheque in it. No one in the Restaurant will assume that you are handing over $300,000. You'll hand it over with a smile that says the war is over between us.

If I'm forced to do business with you, I won't be smiling. I can't trust hoods like you.'

'In that case I want the letter back that Jean wrote to you. Put it in the envelope with the money. If I don't get the letter, you don't get your shoes back. I can't have you using it to blackmail me. It will be easier to maintain honour between thieves if I destroy it.

'Honour! You think I can honour you! You relieve me of almost all the money I have left and talk about honour. If I don't get my 14 million, I'll be blowing the whistle on you and your, crooked dealings so hard that you'll hear it all the way to hell.'

Having vented his spleen, Ray Gasper strode off like a man who's confident that he has the upper hand, but I almost felt sorry for him. Tomorrow he wouldn't even have a whistle to blow.

That night I listened to the recording of the affair on the Cabbage Tree Creek footbridge with DCI Sweetman and the Assistant Commissioner. They were generous with their praise for the part I'd played, but DCI Sweetman pointed out that neither his team nor the forensics lab had found any Parthenium seed at the crime scene or on the shoes.

The Assistant Commissioner laughed and said, 'Parthenium seed was a good sprat to catch a groper or a Gasper with, but tell me   Frank   why   did you carry on and organize the return of the shoes and the handover to you of a cheque for $300,000 at the restaurant on Saturday when you had the confession that will enable us to arrest him tomorrow?'

'Because I needed to protect my undercover status. If I abandoned my plan to extract money from him as soon as he stumbled in to that confession, he'd twig to the fact that I was a policeman and he'd spend the rest of his miserable life plotting my demise from his Jail cell.'

'Of course and we will be circumspect in what we use in court and your status will be sacrosanct even after you retire for the second time.'

'When will that be?'

'When your ersatz Mormons are behind bars.'

Chapter 25

T he arrest of Ray Gasper came as a shock to most of the Serendipity residents since they had supported him so emotionally during the fortnight-long wake before Jane had been laid to rest. None were more shocked, however, than the self-righteous members of the vigilante group who were about to renew their demands that Jean Reid be asked to leave the village because Ray Gasper would never find closure while she was there as a constant reminder of what her nephew had done.

Martha Setright spread it around that Detective Sweetman had got it wrong and the investigation should have been handed over to Inspector Rankin who had enlisted the aid of the whole village when he was investigating the Rosella Lane break-in. He was able to catch Jean Reid's nephew red handed with the stolen goods in his possession. She lauded his arrest of Barnaby Reid as an outstanding example of good police work.

I didn't bother correcting her by pointing out that Inspector Rankin demonstrated good police work when he declined to arrest Barnaby for a crime he didn't commit. Martha Setright wasn't a lady for turning and I suspect that she held on to her perception of the truth even when Gil Rankin arrested Cody and Hank down in Bright at the foot of the snow-covered slopes of Mount Buffalo and had them extradited to Queensland to face Larceny charges associated with a break-in at Serendipity Village.

As a policeman, retired and undercover, I couldn't help but feel satisfied with the part I'd played in securing both the murder and larceny arrests while maintaining my identity in the village as a low-grade public servant. The 1995 event that gave me most pleasure, however, was one that I'd made no contribution to. Jean's book was published and hit the bookshops on a wave of positive reviews. The publisher organized a number of book launches in various venues to maximise the readership, but I suggested another to enable the community here to get to know the real Jean and discover the real qualities of her nephew, Barnaby.

The auditorium was full for the launch at Serendipity. Jean talked about her reason for writing the book and why its pending publication impacted so heavily on Barnaby and caused him to be suspected of theft and murder. To the surprise of all though Barnaby then came to the dais and spoke. With the need for the book's security no longer a problem and his bipolar condition under control Barnaby demonstrated that, like his aunt, he too was a top communicator as he talked about speleology and the underground army headquarters that he'd entered to get the pictures for the book. The round of applause that Barnaby got brought tears to my eyes. He had been rejected by the Village as a crazy thief and murderer and now he was proving to be a catalyst for the healing of Village wounds.

As dramatic as Barnaby's acceptance now was at Serendipity, it was another event that cleared the way for lasting harmony in the Village. It was the brainchild of a couple of members of the philosophy club. They were responding to a call for suggestions for a memorial for Jane Gasper and they had mulled over the provision of some extra facility for the village and they gave thought to the erection of a marble statue. What they came up with, however, was a living memorial to be slotted in to the Serendipity calendar on the first Saturday in September and celebrated each year as Jane Gasper Day.

Preparations for the day are well under way with a broad program of village games in the morning, a Restaurant BBQ at lunch time, followed by singing and dancing in the afternoon backed by the lively music of the Ukulele group. Already an interest in the day has come from outside the village. Fred Walla has offered to supply whatever material is needed for our craft group to make up simple African costumes for some of our residents to wear on the day to highlight our TAWA connection. Jean and I were so taken with the idea that we have offered to organize an exchange of messages of good will on the day between Moyale on the border of Ethiopia and Kenya, and the residents of Serendipity Village in Brisbane.

Chapter 26

Jean and I could settle down to being good neighbours in the best retirement Village in the world but we both know that's not going to be enough for us. We are both ready to give ourselves to each other to let the climaxes of our union dissolve the cares and upsets of daily living. We are in love and yet I am still vacillating. I have a problem.

I have found some comfort in my undercover status in the village because it blocks out the whole of my life as a policeman, but if I joined my life to Jean's I could never keep any secrets at all from her. She knows I'm a policeman, but I have a bit of my life that can't be revealed to anyone without courting dire consequences for me and people I love.

Jean is coming to the conclusion that my love for Nerida, my first wife, was so overpowering that I couldn't extract myself from it. Yes, I did love Nerida but it lasted until death parted us and the years moved on. There was another element of our marriage, however, that required a contract of complete secrecy to cover both of us that was not eliminated by her passing. Thus I can't join my life to Jean's unless I explain to her the full reality of my life with Nerida. She must know that I am always at risk of facing a charge of destroying evidence in a murder investigation to become an accessory after the fact of murder. That is the stumbling block that must be negotiated on the path to true happiness with Jean.

'You are not happy. Frank,' Jean said to me one night as we started our evening meal. 'I'm sorry if I have put any pressure on you to advance our relationship beyond friendship. Obviously, that's not the way you want to go. Your friendship means so much to me and I won't be doing anything to put that in jeopardy.'

'The last thing I want, Jean, is to have you treading on egg shells for fear of upsetting me. Nothing you do could upset me. It's what I've done that's the stumbling block. What I've done must be kept secret. I have to bite the bullet and share that secret with you without nullifying my obligation to keep the secret. I have to find a way to do that.'

'Frank, I don't need to know your innermost secrets! Your life is awash with public demonstrations of your mystery solving. This year you have underlined your genius and you have a lifetime of cases to recall for an enthusiastic public hooked on crime novels. Forget about the odd stumble and immerse yourself in your successes with *Inspector Cole's Cadavers*. I can't wait to read all your cases and if you want me to, I'll edit your manuscripts to get rid of the errors that we two-finger typists are prone to.

I just looked at her and said nothing as the realization jelled in my mind that she had given me the solution to my communication problem with her. Finally I said to her, 'Thank you Jean, I will get started on the cadavers, but the first one I pass on to you will not be published with the Inspector Cole Cases. It won't be published at all. You must take your time reviewing it and making up your own mind about it. I'll call the story *The 5.30 pm Solution* and I'll leave it in your letterbox when I've written it.'

'Of course I'll review anything you write, but Frank, you don't need my acceptance for any decision that you've made in the past or any decisions that you might make in the future for that matter.'

'I need it for the 5.30 pm solution, but let's forget about it now and enjoy each other's company and this beautiful meal,'

She reached across and held my hand. For her the stumble in our relationship had already been negotiated, but she hadn't read the story yet.

Chapter 27

THE 5.30 PM SOLUTION

Dalene and Lee Gallus were in their twenties and Jacinta had just turned eighteen. Jacinta, blond petite and sensitive, took after her mother and dark-haired statuesque Dalene scored a good measure of her father's genes. Lee their brother was like Jacinta though a little taller, but Jacinta's fine boned sensitivity gave him more of a haunted look.

They had been meeting regularly now for a full year in Dalene's flat to bolster each other with a shared revulsion of their step-father. Up to the time of their father's tragic death, their life had been idyllic with the love and security of devoted parents, the material boon of a large child friendly house and the freedom of acreage. Everything changed when the mother, with the welfare of her young family very much in mind, married Henry Fink.

Fink took over one wing of the house for his business activity much of which was carried out at home using the internet. The problem for the young girls, however, was not that they were banned from the business wing but that they were taken in there by Fink and interfered with. Just as frightening as the interference had been were the threats of retribution if they told their mother what was going on. By the time the girls were teenagers the abuse had stopped, but it was shame then that sealed their lips and now as adults they kept quiet knowing the terrible anguish their mother would suffer if she found out what had been happening to them as children.

Lee was not abused in the same way. He suffered disparagement and scorn from a stepfather who saw in him a deficiency of those rugged qualities that would ensure his development into a real man.

Jacinta still lived at Rosemere, the house on acreage, and was able to report to her sister and brother the many instances of mental and physical harassment their mother suffered at the hands pf the monster. Their determination to achieve justice for her was even stronger than the revenge they coveted for themselves.

The final solution was the elimination of Fink, and the strategy finally decided on was one to which each would contribute his or her own professional or personal expertise or circumstantial advantage. They had decided on poisoning quite early in the planning. There was no physical contact with poison and they could be well removed from Rosemere when it was ingested.

It took a little longer, though, to organise the method of ingestion. A cyanide sandwich that could be picked up by anyone would be too risky. Jacinta had Fink under observation for some time before she saw a possible opportunity. The batteries in the remote control were flat. They had been removed from the hand piece and left on the coffee table. New ones had been bought and placed beside the old ones on the table. Fink was liberal with verbal abuse when he found that his wife had mixed the old with the new, but he soon sorted them out by applying each battery to his tongue to determine which ones were charged.

'Hydrocyanic acid,' Dalene said when Jacinta had related the incident. A little hydrocyanic acid on the end of his tongue would do wonders for us.'

Dalene worked for an electroplating firm and she'd been giving some thought to how a poison available to her could be administered.

Months later when Lee, who worked at the power house, was able to give advanced notice of load shedding arrangements to allow a couple of generators to be overhauled, planning for the elimination of Fink shifted into high gear.

Rosemere was in a rural area that was to lose power at 5.30 pm on June 20. Obviously 5.30 pm was the time when everything had to happen. They euphemistically called their whole operation the 5.30 pm solution.

They met as usual on the first Sunday of the month (4th June) and Lee started the ball rolling.

'I'll definitely be on the late shift on the 20th and I'll make sure that Rosemere is blacked out at exactly 5.30. We'll need to synchronize our watches closer to the event.'

'The torch is still in the bottom drawer of his desk,' Jacinta said. 'The three batteries are outside it. He stores them outside the case so they won't go flat. I have three more that I've just about flattened. There won't be a drop of charge left in them when I mix them with the ones in the drawer. When does the poison go on?'

'I'll see to that,' Dalene said. 'Did you get any dates when he's regularly away from the house?'

'Yes, he has PDL on his calendar every third Friday. That's a product distribution lunch. You'll have undisturbed access on June 18.'

'Two days before S Day. I hope it's not too early.'

Shouldn't be, he rarely uses that bottom drawer by the look of what's in it.

'Good,' Dalene said.

'Are we sure he's going to be there. It's not going to be any solution at all if he takes it into his head to be away from Rosemere when the lights go out,' Lee said.

'He'll be there Dalene said flatly. I guarantee that. It makes me sick when I think what I have to do and I don't want to talk about it.'

On Saturday Jacinta and her mother took a taxi to the airport. It had been a stormy week at Rosemere as Fink objected to his wife going off to spend a week with her sister leaving him to fend for himself. He forbad Jacinta to go with her, but Jacinta bore his invective with fortitude and left with her mother boosted by the impending emancipation that the 5.30 pm solution would bring.

Later that afternoon Fink's business phone rang and he hurried in to his office.

'Fink products incorporated here.'

'Dad it's Dalene here. Have they gone?'

'Dalene! Well it's been a long time.'

'Yes, plenty of time to think about things. We had something good going once. It's taken me a few years to realize that that's what I need to recapture.'

Fink couldn't believe what he was hearing.

'You were my favourite, Dalene. I've missed you.'

'I've started to miss you again too, but I couldn't do anything about it while mum and Jacinta were around. It was too risky, especially with Jacinta there.'

The visual memory of Dalene as a little girl added fuel to the virtual proposition of her words and Fink couldn't control his excitement.

'Come over tonight', he said breathing heavily. 'We'll have two weeks together.'

'Oh damn! Dalene said, 'I've got something on tonight I can't get out of and we've got a big job on at the factory and we've been called in to work on Sunday. I'll come Sunday after work. Will you be home then?'

'Are you kidding! Nothing will prize me away from here on Sunday afternoon.'

'Good. I'll be there before 5.30.'

Fink couldn't believe what was happening. A piece of fruit sweet with the swollen ripeness of summer hung on the bare winter branch, his for the picking. It wasn't just his own pleasure that stimulated him. He was a business man and Dalene's passion would be a bell ringer for Fink Products. It hadn't taken him long to grasp the marketing advantages for a girl and woman collation.

Fink products were distributed by a central marketing organization. They were no different from the products that any of the other agents distributed, but the business that each agent generated was marketed under his own label. The regular products advertised gave each agent a legitimate front, but it was the pornography that provided the serious money. It was some time since Fink had produced a hit himself for general distribution, but that was going to change now.

Fink spent Sunday planning what he needed to do and making sure that his equipment was in working order. He put in an eight-hour tape and rolled around on top of the desk to check the camera focus. He switched off the sound. He didn't want anything that was said identifying the location should it get into the wrong hands. The special genius of script writers would provide dialogue and effects that would complement perfectly the impact of his pictures.

At 5.00 pm he wiped what was on the video tape and set it going again. He didn't want to risk switching it on after Dalene arrived. She might well enjoy performing for the camera, some of them did, or she might be turned off by the intrusion. He didn't want that to happen. He closed the blinds shutting out the last rays of a dying winter sun, and he sat down in the arm chair to wait.

It was almost 5.30 and she hadn't arrived. He began to feel anxious. He would feel the frustration keenly if she let him down. When the phone rang, he knew it would be her.

'Dad, it's me. I'm afraid I'm going to be a few minutes late. I said I'd deliver a parcel after work and I've got myself a little lost. I'm in a phone box in Paterson Avenue, but they've ripped the bloody maps out of the book. Could you look up how to get to Connor street from here?'

Fink was relieved she was still coming. 'Hang in there Dalene,' he said reaching for the phone book.

'Now, Lee, Now!' Dalene shouted silently.

'Shit!' Fink exploded.

'What's the matter?' Dalene said simulating concern'

'Bloody lights have gone out.'

'Oh No!' Dalene said smothering relief.

'Wait there, I've got a torch,' he said.

Dalene listened impassively now to the drama of the mixed-up torch batteries and the foul vilification of her mother who didn't have the brains to know that when a battery was flat it was fucking useless. She waited patiently while he went through the business of testing them with his tongue. Finally he had the torch going.

'Now, he said, 'What street did you want?'

But that's as far as he got. Dalene had studied the symptoms of hydrocyanic poisoning and knew that they had achieved their purpose when he was suddenly out of breath and the strangulated noises of his convulsions took over. The abrupt silence of his collapse signified the end and Dalene replaced the phone on the cradle and wept.

Fink's body was discovered two days later by a Telstra technician responding to complaints that Fink products incorporated could not be contacted by phone.

The bright young detective assigned to the case was determined to get a conviction when the coroner indicated hydrocyanic acid as the cause of death. He spent days at the scene of the crime and weeks interviewing people closely associated with Fink.

He'd turned up at the funeral and Dalene could not but think that he had the family under the closest scrutiny. Later it was her firm conviction that she herself was being singled out for particular study. His attention would not have been unwelcome had it not been for the circumstances under which it was given-he was a detective and it was her *idee fixe* to avoid detection. No measure of charm or softly-softly approach on his part would put her off guard.

His attention reached a crisis point for her when he knocked on the door of her flat one evening about a month after the murder.

'May I come in?' he said. 'It's not an official visit,' he added hastily. 'I thought you might want to know how the investigation is progressing.'

His coming like that alarmed her and she had to concentrate on eliminating any agitation from her response.

'We're trying to put all that behind us. It would be enough for us to know that you've charged someone. Is there a suspect?' she added after a slight hesitation.

'Not one we can isolate,' he said choosing his words carefully. 'A number of people could have shared a motive. Dalene, I really do have to talk to you.'

'You'd better come in then,' she said feeling a chill several degrees cooler than the cold night air.

He sat in the armchair opposite her with his slim document case on his lap. 'His real business was pornography, you know. The cheap Fink Enterprise products were just a cover.' He said.

'There were no products of any sort at Rosemere. We knew nothing of his products.'

'Did you know that he produced some of the pornography himself?'

'Where?' she said genuinely surprised.

'In that office of his. There was a hidden camera, it was switched on the night he died.'

'Oh God!' Dalene said.

He studied her carefully. She could have been shocked by the thought of pornography being produced at Rosemere or the switched-on camera could have been a nasty surprise.

'You can see him answer the phone and then there's a blackout, but after a while a torch lights up the map index page of the phone book. The torchlight suddenly goes crazy, When the lights come on again, he's dead. The caller must have heard him having a convulsion on the other end, but did nothing about it.'

Dalene slumped in her chair. She'd called him Dad and he'd called her Dalene in that phone conversation. The detective had her at his mercy and she wanted him to stop harassing her.

'You know who the caller was. Make your arrest and get it over with.'

'There was no sound,' he said. That was switched off. We've no idea who made the call, but the video suggests how the poison might have been taken. If hydrocyanic acid is ingested death comes quickly without an emetic and artificial respiration. The poison must have been taken after the lights went out. I've been over that video a hundred times and there are some significant before and after differences. Before the blackout the table is clear. When the light goes on again, there are three very flat torch batteries on it and of course he now has a torch in his hand. He took some time getting that torch going after the lights went out and he wasn't wandering round looking for it either because we'd have seen the torch coming back from where he found it, It must have been in the drawer. I think he had a number of batteries in there as well and he had to sort out which ones were charged. You can do that by putting your tongue on the terminal. He wouldn't have noticed the moisture on them in the dark. He might have wondered about the almond taste of the hydrocyanic acid, but he would still get the little bite of electricity through the moisture. That's all he was interested in just then.

He knew and her life was over. Dalene sat silently waiting for him to do what he had to do. She let her breathing deepen to try to restore the calmness she wanted as a vehicle for her confession. She would admit what she had done, but no power on earth would draw from her that her brother and sister were also involved. The final solution was that someone must pay for the crime and she would do that, There was no self-pity, just a deep anguish for the grief that would overwhelm her mother.

'There's something I want you to look at,' The detective's soft voice penetrated her turmoil. 'The last thing I want you to do is put you through this, but I need to be certain,'

He unzipped his document case and pulled out a small bundle of white A4 size cards and handed them to her. 'I found these among other photos and negatives in a safe deposit box in a bank. They are part of the Fink estate.

He watched her carefully as she looked at them. The horror registered immediately and the scream died in a convulsion of sobbing as she flung the photos from her.

He was acutely aware of the cruelty he'd inflicted on her. The obscenity of the photos and the wide frightened eyes of the innocent child had shocked him when he first saw them, but there was something about the face of the child that had drawn him back again and again to the photos and he'd sought every opportunity to observe Dalene over the last couple of weeks. He knew now that he was right, but he still had to get her affirmation.

'The child is you, isn't she?'

The almost Imperceptible nod of her head was enough for him. He picked up the scattered photos and stood in front of her. Abandoning his former soft and sympathetic tone, he spoke to her firmly.

'Look at me Dalene, stop sobbing and look at me. I have to have your attention.

She lifted her head and looked at him through the misery of her tears. Suddenly his voice was angry.

'Sub-human bastard,' he shouted with an energy that flowed into the ripping of the photos again and again and again until the small sanitised pieces covered the carpet. He went back to the document case and took out a bulging envelope.

'These are the batteries from the torch and the desk. They might have some cyanic acid still on them. They'll be buried in the deepest garbage tip I can find. I'll be an accessory after the fact.'

She looked at him still in shock, hardly comprehending what he was saying.

'I couldn't bring myself to use those photos in a law court to be stared at by all and sundry.

Help me clean up this mess,' he said bending down to pick up the pieces.

The official verdict was that Fink committed suicide after receiving a mysterious phone call. A little over a year later Dalene Gallus and the detective were married in a ceremony that they both regarded as the ultimate 5.30 solution.

Chapter 28

The brilliant sunset was fading and the first star of the night was confirming its place in the heavens when I knocked quietly on Jean's door. She had read my story and she'd invited me to dinner. I had spent my waiting days convincing myself that I was an unworthy suitor.

Jean was charming, she was a successful novelist, she had the world at her feet and even the Serendipity residents saw her as special as they watched her on TV being interviewed about her book. I remained an antisocial, low grade public servant with nothing to give the community.

Being undercover I was not even associated with any of the police work that went into the arrest of Cody and Hank the ersatz Mormons or taking Ray Gasper into custody.

As soon as Jean opened the door, however, she lifted me right out of my negative mood. She flung her arms around me and kissed my lips.

'I was shedding tears of joy when I finished reading your 5.30 Solution. I was convinced that you wanted us to part ways when you only wanted me to share your burden and your burden was that you refused to arrest a tortured young woman and continue her torture by presenting to the court pornographic photos of her childhood torture at the hands of her evil monster of a stepfather.

Both the evil Fink and your wife Nerida who was the child are dead now, but if some cold case investigator starts up with the mantra that all murderers must be punished, I will leap to the defence of battered and abused children, but let's eat now and talk about where we'll go for our honeymoon.

About the Author

Neill Florence was born in 1932. He is a former High School Principal and English teacher. He acquired his teaching qualifications at Kelvin Grove Teachers College and through External Studies at Qld. University.

On retirement, he joined the Capricorn Coast Writers group in Yeppoon and he has written several novels, a couple of short story collations and his one-act plays have been staged by the Yeppoon Little Theatre.

Neill wrote his latest novel, *Serendipity Murder*, when he and his wife, Ellen, moved into Compton Gardens at Aspley. While Compton Gardens resembles the setting for *Serendipity Murder* the characters are entirely fictional.

Life at Compton Gardens is busy and fulfilling and with five children, eleven grandchildren, and three great-grandchildren beyond the village, life is also interesting and absorbing.

www.ingramcontent.com/pod-product-compliance
Lightning Source LLC
Chambersburg PA
CBHW020640250626
47154CB00008B/2756